POWER OF THE *Light*

Liliane Grace

Published by Grace Productions
Romsey, Victoria, Australia

https://lilianegrace.com

Text copyright © Liliane Grace 2020

A catalogue recording for this book is available from the National Library of Australia

ISBN 978-0-6485624-5-0

Cover design © Jeremy Strong, Shevek Creative
Typesetting by Jeremy Strong, Shevek Creative
Jeremy@shevekcreative.com

Typeset in 11pt Minion Variable Condensed and Avenir Next

Printed on demand by Ingram Spark

"You never change things by fighting the existing reality. To change something, build a new model that makes the existing model obsolete."
– **Buckminster Fuller**

"All tissues can be regenerated, all hurts can be forgiven and all lives can be brought into wholeness."
– **Rohan Callander, Detox Specialist**

"Wisdom is looking back on your life and realising that every single event was nothing but fuel that you can use in your rocket ship to fulfil your mission, and anything in your life that you do not see with gratitude and love is your lie, it's your baggage and it weighs your spaceship down and you can't launch. Anything you see with love you turn into light, and light is your fuel and you take off."
– **Dr John Demartini,** *The Cosmogonic Cycle – Spirit, Energy, Matter*

"This book was amazing. I thoroughly enjoyed reading every word of the adventures of Nathan as he learns many valuable lessons while his dad goes through the tough times of cancer. The lessons this book has on healthy eating and having a healthy mind are well worth the read and should be taught to everyone. I would also recommend this book not just for the fact that it has great life lessons but also that it is an entertaining read and had me wanting to read it all in one sitting!"
- **Jasper, age 14**

"I really liked this book! *Power of the Light* has a great message and lessons that are really needed right now. I particularly liked that Nathan is learning this stuff at a young age."
- **Luna, age 17**

"This touching story shows how our thoughts and emotions, as well as the food we put into our bodies, affects our health. It dives into how different emotions can have a direct impact on our health, sometimes without us even realizing. It is a beautiful story for all ages about family, love, and the power of forgiveness through the eyes of a very awakened 13-year-old boy named Nathan, and how he changes his thoughts through his father's illness, his family's struggles, and a dreamworld that brings new awareness to light."
– **Dr Robert Morse N.D., D.Sc., M.H.,**
www.dmhhc.com

"*Power of the Light* is a story with a message of hope for families who are faced with fear of the unknown – specifically when a family member is diagnosed with cancer.

"Having lived through a 'terminal' cancer diagnosis myself, and due to the conscious lifestyle choices I made that set me on a path to optimal health, I can relate to the importance of the messages in *Power of the Light*. Since my cancer diagnosis, I have now been actively following a raw vegan lifestyle for 20 years and, at the age of 64, I set a World Record for running 366 consecutive marathons while running around Australia. Now, at the age of 70, I am still running marathons due to my ongoing conscious lifestyle which keeps me in a state of optimal health.

"I believe that *Power of the Light* is a timely story with a positive message for all humanity, a story that shows the power of positive thinking, the power of light through love, and the power of raw living foods."
– Janette Murray-Wakelin, Author, *Raw Can Cure Cancer*, https://rawveganpath.com

"While *Power of the Light* is written as a novel it most certainly represents hundreds, if not thousands, of real-life alternative healing testimonials. This story is inspiring and thought provoking, and seems to parallel my own healing journey with breast cancer. I applied the energetic 'Power of the Light': eating organic raw fruits and vegetables and balancing the mental, emotional and spiritual aspects of my life by addressing unfinished business. The result was that I was able to repair, regenerate and restore my body, mind

and overall health. The journey was profoundly intense, yet simple, non-toxic, non-invasive and more importantly – incredibly effective! In my opinion, cancer and so many other diseases are only symptoms of a body that is out of harmony physically, mentally, emotionally and spiritually. Once given the proper tools, my body completely healed."
– **Linda Christina Beauregard, author,** *I Gave Myself Cancer, I Can Take It Away – Alternatives Brought Me Back To Life*

"An excellent message that needs to be shared with the community. I get a little frustrated when I hear so much 'stuff' on the media about the latest research and treatments for cancer. Fear is the biggest killer, not the tumour. I have worked with people who have cancer and although I recommend high doses of nutrition, I also know that the mind work is half the battle. Love your disease: it is a message to make changes – a lot better than fighting it or hating it."
– **Elaine Stoeckel, naturopath**

"Adversity can strike in anyone's life and if it does, you have two choices: either you lie down and wallow in your sadness and helplessness and submit to the disease, or you work through it and head for a better life. In *Power of the Light*, Liliane Grace accurately depicts the devastation that comes to a family with a cancer diagnosis, and the various responses that each one brings to the situation.

"When I was diagnosed with cancer I was initially shocked because I thought I was young and healthy. The confusion of the sudden diagnosis and the decisions I needed to make about the necessary treatment created great pressure as I also had a family to care for. I came to understand that I needed healing not just for my body, but also in my spirit and in my soul.

"I am grateful for the body's wonderful ability to heal itself when given the correct nutrition and mindset. Liliane offers the keys to handling adversity through several thought-provoking ideas that will enable readers to live life to the best of their ability. A simple-to-read, easy-to-understand, difficult-to-put-down, must-have book."
– **Yvonne Chamberlain, author of** *Why Me? Kicking Cancer and other life changing stuff!*

"What a refreshing honour it was to read your latest novel. I thought the cancer story was very honest. The automatic option is to choose chemo and radiotherapy, which can do awful things to your body. It is while you are at your most vulnerable, waiting for the chemo to do its thing, that your mind explores options, reasons, what we take into our bodies, relationships, and the meaning of life. You have covered all of this so nicely. Cancer can be seen as an opportunity, not a death sentence. That is how I saw it at the time, and still do."
– **Jennifer Mannell, physiotherapist and cancer conqueror**

"I loved it! I think it's exciting to be able to take ownership of everything we create, not in the form of blame or self-hate but total empowerment."
– Amber Mason, counsellor

"Everyone needs to read this book. I was sad when I had finished – I could have read on and on... The wisdom is precious. I will highlight it so I can remember the process. I laughed to myself when I realised the words 'creator' and 'reactor' have the same letters in them. That was my biggest pivotal moment in the book. I would have no hesitation recommending this book to my entire community. The concepts are phenomenal. I've been on this spiritual journey for 35 years but it changed the way I look at the world. Totally amazing."
– Julie Lewin, Medical Intuitive and author of *The Art of Self-Healing*

"Liliane has the most amazing gift of sharing profound lessons through story. *Power of the Light* is an engaging, thought-provoking read that is so perfect in times of uncertainty, for young people and adults alike. Liliane shares an empowering message of taking control of our own health and destiny, something we all would benefit from doing more of!"
– Stephanie Kakris, Creator of 'Higher Wisdom' Parenting Oracle Cards

DEDICATION

This book is dedicated to the many courageous women, men and children who are diagnosed with cancer and choose to trust the healing power of nature above medical intervention, and, in particular, to those among them who shared their inspiring stories with me. I would also like to thank the authors and educators who have woken me up to our body's ability to heal, especially Don Tolman and Dr Robert Morse.

Thanks, also, to a writing student of mine many years ago whose characters were in trouble. In coaching him, I stumbled upon the possibility of 'the Power of the Light'.

I hope this story enlightens *your* world.

SPECIAL NOTE

I am launching this novella in 2020, during the period of the COVID-19, a phenomenon that has literally stopped the world. The greatest infections are probably fear and misinformation, and while the metaphor of the 'Reactors' in my story may seem simplistic, I invite you to check how much you are influenced by the fear and opinions of those around you, or by the mainstream media.

The information I share at the back of this book about health and healing will conflict with many popular views; I hope that it inspires you to investigate further and to take full responsibility for your own health and healing.

CONTENTS

PROLOGUE

Nathan was running late for his own birthday party. He could hear all the voices in the living room – his parents and grandparents and a few other rellies – but he was so caught up in the game he was playing that he couldn't drag himself away. And anyway, Brett hadn't arrived yet. When you're about to be given a whole lot of dodgy gifts and have everyone looking at you and asking you questions, you need a friend by your side. Especially someone you've known since Grade 3, who has hung out with your family for years and can overlook their flaws.

To be honest, Nathan wouldn't even be having this family party if he was one of those guys with a whole footy team of friends, but since starting high school he still only had Brett. He got on with most of the other guys but he wasn't exactly *in* with them. They'd pick him for their team because he was fast and reasonable with a ball; but then they'd stop picking him because half the time when they needed him, he'd be gazing in the wrong direction, totally caught up in his own thoughts. Or they'd be sitting in the common room laughing and joshing and ribbing people, and one minute Nathan would be right with them, and the next, he'd be off in some daydream again... In the end, he was often ignored and left to himself.

Nathan's mother, Prue, who made friends wherever she went, had been troubled to find that her son did not yet have the football team set of mates, so she'd dumped this big family gathering on him. She'd come home on Friday night from the supermarket with bags of chips and soft drink and mud cakes and jelly snakes, all in an effort to make him feel popular and special, but he wished she hadn't. Which made him feel bad. He didn't like being unappreciative but he'd have much preferred an expansion pack for his game and a sleepover at Brett's house.

Somebody laughed uproariously in the living room and the doorbell rang; in the same moment, he achieved the next level game milestone he was after. So no more excuses to hide out in his bedroom. He logged off and took a deep breath in readiness for joining the fray.

"... get the birthday boy out of his den," his mother was saying as he appeared in the doorway. Everyone turned to look at him and began with the happy birthdays. All four grandparents plus some adult cousins with their brood of little-kid cousins – he did a quick mental check on his bedroom door and was pretty sure he'd closed it, and – thank God – Brett, who was giving him the comical raised-brows, starey-eyed 'You'll pay!' expression.

Nathan's father emerged from the kitchen with a tray of delicious-smelling, golden sausage rolls, but before he could grab one, both grandmothers were bearing down on him with crackly-paper presents. He sank onto the sofa.

Grandma was a knitter – of prickly jumpers that you couldn't wear out in public, and warm socks that were too thick for your shoes. This jumper was green with a purple V-neckline. Brett immediately raved about it and Grandma promised to make him one too. "He's teasing you, love," Grandad said drily.

Nan's specialty was books, and her standard gift was two novels and something unpredictable. She was usually pretty spot-on with the novels because she asked her local bookstore for popular teen titles. The other book would be about the solar system or how to raise chickens or something random like that; this time it was on Egyptian history. She leaned in with a soft, scented cheek for a kiss, and Pa raised a hand from an armchair.

Nathan was finally digging into the sausage rolls when his Aunt Cherry arrived. Immediately he looked at his father. Matt had glanced up as his sister entered; now he was smoothly picking up platters that needed refilling and retreating with them to the kitchen. Nathan and his mother looked from the closing kitchen door to Cherry, who was smiling brightly at everyone. Prue shrugged; they'd become used to the silent feud between Matt and Cherry. In fact, his whole father's family was prone to conflict and arguments. Grandma tried to be the healing balm but her son was always either clashing with his father or his sister. This was another reason why Nathan wished Prue had not organised a birthday party. It was just a question of time before someone quarrelled.

"The prawns!" Prue exclaimed, jumping up. "Hello

Cherry, welcome. I'll be right back," and she disappeared into the kitchen after her husband.

Cherry located Nathan and came to give him a hug and an envelope and a sunny smile. "You don't have to open it now," she said. "I thought that rather than giving you stuff, especially since I don't know what you like nowadays, I'd take you out to the movies or something – your choice when you're ready."

"Thanks!" He slid the envelope under his plate.

Prue returned with the prawns and Matt reappeared soon after and was even quite friendly with his sister, though he redirected the conversation when she asked if he'd had any articles published lately. Things were pretty calm, if noisy, for a while, until Cherry started talking about this fascinating doco she had seen about how governments were so corrupt that they were even governing illegally, but there were things people could do to get themselves out of that system. Immediately, Grandad said "Rubbish" and talked right over her, and this time Matt sided with his dad. Soon after that, Cherry remembered that she had double-booked, and she left, taking some of the sunshine with her.

Brett started leafing through the book on Egyptian history and showing Nathan pictures of their gods with falcon heads and multi-coloured wings. "Straight out of our games!" he crowed.

Matt leaned in for a look. "You mean your games come straight out of Egyptian mythology."

"Didn't you write an article once about something to do with the gods?" Prue asked, proffering the platter of prawns.

"I did," he said, helping himself. "Fascinating culture. I wrote a few about ancient Egypt, actually. One on their gods and one about the legal and financial independence that Egyptian women enjoyed."

"So two articles about gods." Prue grinned.

Matt bowed in her direction. "A very enlightened culture, actually. They negotiated one of the earliest peace treaties on record, and had one of the first recorded labour strikes."

Nathan looked at the book with more interest. It seemed that his Nan had picked a good one this time.

Prue brought out the birthday cake and Nathan suffered through the song and wishes and calls for a speech, which he ignored. As he bent to blow out the candles, he noticed that his father was cradling his stomach in both hands and frowning down at the table top while everyone around him smiled and laughed and joked. Suddenly Matt rose, blurting, "Bad prawn I think!" and dashed out.

He was gone for a long time and it wasn't until a few months later that Nathan realised that was when everything began to change.

Chapter 1

THE NEWS THAT NOBODY WANTED

When he came home from school there was a funny feeling in the house. It was quiet, but it was usually quiet, so that was nothing new. His dad worked alone in a tiny study at the back of the house and could type away even if a bomb had gone off next door, as his mum often said, and she worked in the city and wouldn't be home for a while.

Nathan dropped his school bag in his bedroom and walked to the kitchen. His mother had made him egg sandwiches for lunch and he hated egg sandwiches so he'd given them to Eric and now he was starving. He pulled the fridge door open and that was when he heard it, a little noise like a sob. He paused, listening, but it was quiet again so he turned back to the fridge. There it was: last night's lasagne.

Food, fork, and he was on his way to the lounge room to watch TV when he heard it again. And this time that was definitely a sob. Someone was crying.

Nathan stopped again and cocked his head, listening. "Dad?" he called out, and the sobbing noise stopped.

Instead, there was a murmur of voices and then a door opening and his mother said, "Nathe?"

"What are you doing home?" Nathan asked, turning toward her voice. She came around the corner from her bedroom and he saw that she had taken off those crazy-heeled shoes she wore to work but was still wearing her blue suit, although it didn't look as sharp as it had that morning; it looked crumpled and the skirt was twisted. But it was her red eyes he noticed in particular, her red eyes and mussed-up hair.

"Hey, Nathe," she said, and wrapped her arms around him, pressing him close. She was warm and smelt faintly of mint. He wriggled a bit; the container of lasagne was still in his hand and he didn't want to drop it. "How was school?" she asked through a sniff.

"Okay," he said. "Are you sick?"

"No!" she exclaimed in a strange voice, and loosened her grip on him so she could take a step back and look at him. "Why do you say that?"

"Well, you're home early and you sound funny..."

"Oh." His mother twisted her wedding ring for a moment, staring at the ground. Then she looked directly at him and took his hand. "It's Dad, love. He's sick."

Brett would already be watching at his place and they liked watching at the same time so they could call each other to talk about stuff. "I'll eat this and then I'll go see him," Nathan said, taking a step backwards, toward the lounge room.

"Okay," she replied, without moving, just standing there, and her expression was so sad that he stopped where he was too. Tears were gathering in her eyes and spilling over.

"Why are you crying?"

"It's not just – a cold," she spurted out, in a voice that was snuffly with crying. "It looks bad."

"What sort of bad?" Nathan asked, but he didn't really want to know.

She shook her head, unable to speak, wiping the back of her hand across her nose, and crying more and more.

Nathan walked to his parents' bedroom with all his thoughts on pause. Some part of him knew he was still holding the container of lasagne but it was as if his feelings were in slow-mo too. He was a walking person and that was all. He walked around the doorway into the bedroom and saw his father sitting on the side of the bed with his head in his hands. His father was in slow-mo too. Very gradually he turned his head towards Nathan, and very gradually his strained expression was replaced by a weak smile.

"Hey, mate," he said.

Nathan put the lasagne container on the dresser. "What's wrong?"

"They're not sure yet, but it's not looking good." And now his father's eyes were filling with tears – his *father*, a man who never cried, and he was reaching out for Nathan and pulling him close and making big noisy sobs.

He is walking along a street, vaguely aware of more streets on one side of him and fields on the other side.

It's a lovely, sunshiny, blue-sky day. The air feels warm and there's something like hay in the fields. He walks along, humming a song.

The next minute he's in a house with lots of people, a happy family of people, who are all talking at once and coming and going with doors opening and closing and stuff happening. A large man offers him some food and then someone calls, 'It's starting!' and everyone goes into the lounge room to watch something on TV. He goes with them, finding a seat on the floor because the room is so crowded. It's a really old-fashioned TV, like the sort his parents had when they were little. He wonders about that.

The screen flickers and crackles and then a frowning man with thick brown hair appears and makes an announcement.

*"In times like these we must be realistic," he says heavily, and the people in the room all stir a bit and murmur. "The time for dreaming is **over**. These are emergency measures. It looks serious because it **is**. Please adjust your picture to **match the facts**."*

Nathan looks around him at all the people who are watching the TV. Most of them are frowning.

"You see," someone says, "I told you."

The man on TV begins to make exactly the same announcement all over again. Somewhere in the house a door opens and a voice calls, "Yoohoo! Where are you?"

"In here!" someone yells, and a moment later a woman wearing a glorious orange-patterned dress

comes bursting into the room like a lovely warm breeze.

"You missed it," someone says.

"Oh hooey," she replies, with a quick shrug. She has a dimple in one cheek that makes her whole face light up. "That message is just hooey."

"Don't say that," someone says. "These are dark times. We need to be careful."

"Hooey!" the smiley orange person says again. "Hooey, hooey, hooey!"

Someone echoes the frowning TV man: "The time for dreaming is over. You can't ignore the facts, Rada."

"The time for dreaming is just starting," Rada contradicts, leaning forwards with an intense smile. She straightens up. "So – who's with me?"

The room erupts into chatter. Everyone is deciding.

"You can't do this!" another person says. "It's too dangerous. You'll be found."

"Why?" she asks brightly. "Will you give me away?"

The person stares at her angrily. "I might have to."

"I'll take that risk," she says with a toss of her head. "Okay, who's coming?"

Bit by bit the room divides into those who remain sitting (frowning) and those who stand up (smiling) and go toward the woman called Rada. Nathan hesitates. Come where? he wonders. Rada notices him and beckons. "Come on, Nathan," she calls, "you're with us!"

He gets up in relief, and follows the people who are following her.

"You'll be found!" the someone calls after them, and Rada laughs.

Nathan finds himself smiling, warming, as he follows her, and he sees that the people in this group are all smiling; it's as if they have a secret.

"Chuff, chuff!" Rada sings, the way his mother did when he was little, pretending to be a steam train so he would let her take him to bed. Rada is leading them through the house and across a field, only this time the sky is really grey and overcast and it feels lower, somehow. Nathan is so busy staring at the clouds that, before he knows it, they're in a room with mirrors all around the walls, like a dance studio, and Rada is standing in the centre of the room and smiling at everyone and saying, "Okay, everyone, this is It. You've chosen and now is when it starts."

And then her smile fades just a little and she says in a quieter voice, "You've all met Reactors before and you will again. They are here to stay, folks. But you are making a choice to be Creators, and that means Serious Magic. The thing is," and her voice lowers even more, "this calls for more courage and more strength than anything you've ever done before. Are you up for it?"

"Will it be dangerous?" a girl asks. She's wearing blue overalls and chewing gum.

Rada smiles again and when she speaks, she is almost as boisterous as when she first appeared. "Not nearly as dangerous as they'd like us to think!"

"But tricky, right?" a thinnish young man asks.

*"Tricky is the word," Rada agrees. "Appearances are **very** seductive."*

The group talks among themselves for a moment, and Rada's eyes turn to Nathan's. She smiles at him quite intently.

When it's time to leave, it's very dark outside. They almost can't see a thing. Nathan reaches out a hand to feel his way and whacks it on something hard. He gasps and opens his eyes.

The bathroom door. It was closed, and the house was silent. Except for a faint moaning sound coming from his parents' bedroom.

Chapter 2
COLD-FRONT-DAD

The house always seemed to be full of people these days. There was Mrs Oldham, who was retired so she had the time to keep popping in the back door with 'bits and pieces to cheer Dad up', as she'd say to Nathan, winking brightly as she put a dish of cake or lamingtons or jam rolls on the table. Then she'd turn very serious, asking gravely, "How is he today, the poor love?" Nathan would shrug and mumble, "The same," and her face would cloud over and she'd look terribly worried for a moment, and then suddenly she'd brighten up again and say in a falsely cheerful voice, "I'm sure he'll come good any day now! Any day now..." And they'd both know she was speaking rubbish, so Nathan would mumble something else and get out of the kitchen, calling to his mum that Mrs O was there.

And lots of family visited, including people he hadn't seen for ages, like his Aunt Cherry, even though she and his dad still hadn't properly made up after their last set of arguments. But Cherry was there all the time lately, smiling cheerily at him and bringing big jugs of homemade vegetable juice for her sick brother. *Vegetable* juice! Fruit juice he could understand, but juicing carrots and beetroot and cabbage and stuff like that? Weird. She'd always give him a sip and he'd wrinkle his nose in anticipation of something terrible, though it was never as bad as he expected. And she'd bring books and magazines with names like "Juice Fasting for Health" and "Cancer Recovery from A-Z."

Aunt Cherry would spy the cake or lamingtons and frown a bit and say something like, "This is one of the culprits," to his mum, who would exclaim, "Oh *really*! How can a piece of cake hurt?" And Aunt Cherry would very earnestly insist that Mum and Dad read her books and articles because so-and-so had had exactly the same type of cancer and now he was okay or she was doing fine... and Nathan's mum would smile politely and say, "I know you mean well, Cherry, but he just doesn't trust that alternative stuff.." and then, at Cherry's stricken expression, "Oh, leave it on the table – I'll have a look at it later;" and the pile in the corner of the kitchen table would grow, but Nathan never saw his mum or dad reading any of it.

Both sets of Grandparents kept dropping in, too – his mother's parents, Nan and Pa, making brief visits to bring casseroles and cheer their daughter up (which never worked because those were usually the days she broke down crying), and his father's parents, Grandma and Grandad, who would disappear into Dad's bedroom for ages. Occasionally he'd hear a raised voice – usually Grandad's, and then his grandfather would storm out, banging the front door behind him, but Nathan never knew what had been said. Not that he wanted to know.

The minister would come by occasionally to "bring comfort and remind you to have faith". "Faith in what?" his mother snapped once. "In prayer," the minister had replied, taken aback. "Do you really think that pleading to a – a mythical being is going to make any difference whatsoever?" she had retorted. The minister had hesitated and then simply nodded, and with flashing eyes she'd told him that they appreciated his concern but they were putting their faith in *Science*, not Spirituality, in something of *Substance*. (It was not as if they had asked him to drop in so really he was meddling, thanks to Grandma.) But he still came by occasionally, or a card would turn up in the mail with encouraging messages like, *"and He told me, 'My grace is sufficient unto you, for My strength comes to perfection where there is weakness... For when I am weak, then I am strong." – Corinthians, 12, 9-10.*

"Yeah, right!" Nathan's mother would exclaim in disgust, and she'd toss the card in the bin. But sitting at the table eating cornflakes, Nathan could just read bits of the message if he cocked his head on one side, and the curious words, 'For when I am weak, then I am strong,' stayed with him, revolving in his mind like a song that had become stuck there.

What with all these comings and goings their house always seemed to be full of people, crowding up the kitchen and hovering in the lounge room or on the front porch, speaking in whispers. It was just as well they came with food because his mother had virtually stopped cooking, she was so stressed and busy, but the sight of a car out the front when he got home from school, or the sound of quiet voices in the house when he stepped in, were beginning to get Nathan down. He just wished they'd all go away because those people being there was a sign that everything was different and wrong.

And yet when they were gone it was even worse; then the place was so quiet and still... Not with the normal-life quietness it used to have when Dad was hard at work in his study, but in a new way that made you walk through it on guard, listening, alert... alert for where his dad was, so that he could go somewhere else to escape the personal cloud his father seemed to travel under these days. Nathan could almost feel him coming into a room; it was as if the temperature grew colder as his father approached. He started to joke about it in his own mind – oh no, here comes Cold-Front-Dad, bringing drizzle and grey clouds...

It felt mean to think of his father like that, but that was exactly what it was like. Ever since the operation his father had become a slow, heavy figure shuffling between the bedroom and the bathroom. Sometimes his cloud took over the whole lounge room – Nathan's mother would tell his dad to go in there and watch TV to 'get his mind off it', but whenever Nathan came in he wasn't watching, just lying on the couch and staring into the distance. It didn't feel okay to change the channel, though, so Nathan would drift out again.

He started to spend more time outside, or at his mate Brett's house, where it wasn't so dark and heavy and life seemed normal – apart from everyone going all serious as soon as he arrived, and asking gravely, "How's your dad doing?" He'd lie, to get them to change the subject: "Much better!" and they'd all look relieved and ask about school or soccer instead. And then the Dad-cloud, which could infect other people's places, and even school, would lift and life would be normal again.

The cloud was like the dirty cancer-stain they had told him about on the x-ray pictures of his dad's bowel. It was spreading through everything, infecting everything.

It is night. There is a sharp wind, and people hurry along the streets with their heads bowed, or huddle together in doorways, whispering and glancing over their shoulders. Nathan is following someone who had caught his sleeve and given him a meaningful look. They walk quickly, feeling people's eyes on them as they pass, and suddenly a door opens on their right and they pass through it, and they are in the mirrored room again.

Rada is writing on the glass and there is a small circle around her. She turns back to face the group and catches sight of Nathan, and a radiant smile bursts onto her face, her cheeky dimple appearing at once. He smiles back, relaxing.

"Now here's the thing," she says to the group, and they are instantly quiet, listening. "It's all just an energy game. The reason the Reactors are taking over is because that takes less energy. You see? It's like going down a slide – much easier than climbing up, right?"

The people nod, and Nathan nods with them. Of course. That's obvious.

"Focused Creation takes much more energy. **Heaps** of energy," Rada continues, looking at each person intently. "It's like going against gravity. It's **much** easier to give up and join the Reactors. Much."

"That's why they're taking over so quickly," someone says with a worried frown.

"Are you Reacting to that?" Rada asks quietly, and the person's eyes widen in realisation. A titter passes through the group.

"But how do you get enough energy to resist them?" someone else asks. It's the girl in the blue overalls.

Rada shakes her head. "Never resist," she says. "That only makes them stronger. **Create**."

"But how do you get enough energy to create?" the thinnish man next to Nathan demands. "If creating is so hard…"

"Want it," Rada says with a brilliant smile.

They are in the TV room again. The frowning man with thick brown hair is making another Announcement.

"You must trust the evidence of your senses," he is saying. "If a woman has a different skin colour to yours, is she the same as you? No! She is different. If a man has different customs, is he the same? No! You know that is true."

"Yes, that's true," someone murmurs.

"If you are weak, you cannot be strong," TV man continues in a stern tone of voice. "If you are strong, you are not weak. You know this is true. Trust your reactions and your logic. If you feel fear, then the thing is a cause for concern and you should shield yourself from it or fight it." The man frowns and the camera zooms in on his face. "A war is coming," he says gravely.

These words appear on the screen: TRUST YOUR REACTIONS. SHIELD OR FIGHT.

Somewhere in the house a door opens and a voice calls, "Yoohoo! Where are you?"

"In here," someone calls back, and a moment later Rada enters in her orange patterned dress.

"You're not listening to more of that hooey, are you?" she exclaims, with a glance at the screen.

*"It makes sense," someone mutters. "We have to trust the evidence of our senses. They offer **proof**. You're talking – magic! Mumbo-jumbo."*

"What about love?" Rada asks, flinging her arms out. "Do you believe in love? You can't touch or see love!"

"She's right," someone says.

"But it's so much easier to believe in things we can see and feel!"

*"Of course!" Rada leaps suddenly onto a table, and stands there, staring down at them. "Remember, Creation takes energy – **lots**." She drops lightly off the table and squats, gazing up at them. Nathan thinks of the slide: difficult to climb up, easy to slide down.*

"But what if we don't have enough energy to fight the darkness?" someone demands.

Rada strides to the wall and flicks the light switch off. Instantly the room is pitch black. Nathan strains to see something, anything.

"How do you eliminate the dark?" Rada asks, her voice ringing out. In a second, the room is sunny with light again and she is beaming at them from where she stands by the wall, her hand still poised over the switch. "You don't fight the darkness; you just **turn on the light.**"

"A piece of cake!" someone says sarcastically, and Rada laughs.

Her gaze comes to rest on Nathan and she says it again. "You don't go to war with the darkness; you **switch on the light.**"

You switch on the light, he thinks, and he thinks it over and over, so that when the dark shapes loom close and fear chokes in his gut and rises to his throat, he screams those words, "**Switch on the light!**"

– and suddenly the room *was* light, and his mother was leaning over him with a concerned expression in her bleary eyes.

"Are you okay?" she asked, and she put a warm hand against the side of his face and held it there, tenderly, while the two worlds gradually separated, and the other one melted away.

Chapter 3

THE REACTORS TAKE OVER

No one was parked outside the house. Good.

Nathan dropped his bike to the ground, pushed the front door open and headed in, looking for his mother. Brett was waiting outside, resting on his bike. There was a teacher's strike tomorrow so they had a plan: a sleepover at Brett's and a night of gaming. He was already thinking about his character as he headed towards his parents' bedroom. He'd been a troll lately, but he was sick of that. Brett's character was this very cool warrior with rippling muscles and a collection of pretty sick weaponry. He wanted that, too.

"You and Nathe will be better off without me," his father's muffled voice said wearily, and Nathan froze, fist raised, about to knock on their door.

"Don't talk like that!" his mother hissed, but her voice was cut off by the horrible sound of his father spewing. Nathan's arm dropped to his side. He stood still, as if paralysed.

His mother was murmuring soothingly while his father retched. After a few minutes the bed springs creaked and Nathan's father sighed heavily. Something thudded softly onto the floor. Something rustled.

"I'm serious, Prue," he said weakly, and it was so quiet that Nathan could even hear the long, slow, out-breath he gave. "I'm screwing everything up. You're doing well. Let's face it: you're already supporting us. My income has been going from bad to worse."

"That's irrelevant!" his mother exploded, and she sounded slightly hysterical. "Who cares? It doesn't matter at all! I love my work and you love yours and who cares? Don't be such a bloody Neanderthal! So what if I support us? So bloody what!"

"I feel like a waste of space," Nathan's father muttered. "I want you to hear me." The mattress and sheets rustled again. "This cursed disease is killing me. You have to face up to it. But you'll be all right. I want you to go on, Prue. You deserve a great life. Let yourself find someone else."

"*Shut up!* If you weren't so sick, I'd hit you."

It was silent for a moment. Nathan exhaled quietly. He took one soft step backwards. And then another. And then he struck that stupid creaking board. He turned and walked back outside really quickly.

Brett was riding in circles on the front lawn with no hands. He saw Nathan and stopped. "Okay?"

Nathan shrugged. "Nah. Can't find her. Better not."

Brett cocked his head. He was looking past Nathan, over his shoulder, back into the house. Nathan turned around and there was his mother, with a stricken expression.

"Nathe," she said intently. "Were you outside the door for long?"

"Nah," he said. And shrugged again. "I was just coming to ask you if I can go to Brett's tonight. No school tomorrow – teacher's strike."

"Of course," she said, and she looked relieved. She gave Brett a strained smile. "Hi Brett. How are things?"

"Okay," he replied, landing on one foot. "How's Mr C?"

"Pretty down, actually," she said, and her lip wobbled. "At the moment."

"Oh."

None of them spoke. It was warm. A bird sang out.

Prue was pulling herself together. "Give my regards to your parents."

"Okay," Brett said.

She looked at Nathan, as if she was trying to remember something. "What do you need? To take?"

"Nothing. It's okay," Brett intervened. "He doesn't need anything."

"All right then." She came forward and wrapped her arms around Nathan, burying her face in his hair. "Take care. I love you."

"I know," he mumbled, hugging her back.

"And Dad loves you. A lot."

"I know. Will I...?"

"No... He just threw up. He's feeling crappy."

"Tell him...

"I will. You have a good time. Take care."

"I will."

"I love you," she said again. The tears were spurting from her eyes now. She didn't even try to stop them.

Nathan seized his bike off the path, leapt onto the seat and rode away hard. There was one part of him bursting into tears along with his mother, and another part that was mad as hell. He rode so fast that it took Brett a block and a half to catch up with him.

The whole place is at war. He can hardly believe how serious it's become in such a short time. They sit in the mirrored room and hear shouting and explosions and high-pitched sirens outside. Rada is writing on the glass in big letters: 'LOOK IN THE MIRROR'.

The door crashes open and somebody bursts in. It's the thinnish man. There's blood trailing from a gash on his face and his clothes are ripped and dirty. "You have to hide!" he yells. "They're coming!"

Rada turns away from the mirror and looks at him thoughtfully.

"Are you paying attention?" he screams. "It's over! You can't keep this charade up! They know where we are!"

"Really?" she asks.

His head whips from the door to her face to the faces of the few people sitting on the floor. His eyes are wild and staring. "They've got monsters," he whispers. "I saw one… pick an old woman up and… toss her… They've got magic. The ground was melting

- I saw it! Dissolving into smoke. People were falling into it. It's horrible!"

"What should we do?" a plump woman asks gaspingly. Her hand is pressed to her lips, eyes wide.

"We've got to fight," the girl in the overall says firmly. She stands up.

"Fight what?" Rada asks.

"The Reactors!"

"If you do, you'll become one," Rada states simply. "What you resist, persists. The more you fight it, the stronger it gets."

"So, what are we supposed to do? Nothing?" The thinnish man starts pacing. He is still panting.

Rada looks at Nathan. "What do you think?"

He is startled. He raises his shoulders, shaking his head slightly. He has no idea. The situation looks hopeless.

"Hmmm," she says.

"Rada!" the thinnish man says urgently, "we've got to **do** something!"

The plump woman rises suddenly, pulling her children up with her. Her body is like folds of jelly, all quivering. "I'm going. I'm sorry. I can't do this. They say that as soon as you surrender everything is okay again - they don't turn on you. I'm going to surrender. I have children!"

Rada gazes at her tenderly. "Smoke and mirrors," she says.

"What?" the woman snaps. "You're speaking in riddles." She is gathering her children close to her *large, soft body, ready to leave.*

Nathan looks at the words Rada had inscribed on the glass.

"You're fighting smoke and mirrors," Rada says. "What you resist, persists."

"I don't understand!" The woman begins to herd her children in front of her towards the door. Their eyes are big and frightened.

"What does 'look in the mirror' mean?" Nathan asks.

"Ah," says Rada. She turns to Nathan with a gentle smile, as if they are in the middle of a lesson at school and not in the middle of a ferocious war with Reactors. "What do you see when you look in the mirror?"

"Myself," he replies, puzzled.

"Exactly," she says.

"Rada, would you please speak some sense!" the thinnish man explodes.

*"Their greatest weapon is our self-rejection," she replies. "Those Reactors take the form of whatever we hate in ourselves. There is no enemy out there! They are **us**, the Reactors are us!"*

The room is silent. Everyone is thinking about this.

*"You have to understand," Rada is looking at them with intense focus. "Those creatures are not separate things from you! They are reflections, projections – ideas that have spiralled out of control! **Your** ideas. And when you fight them, they get stronger. That's what they want, don't you see? They want you to*

React. They want you to reject yourself because then you become one of them: **their power grows when you hate yourself.** *But you have another option. You can choose to love yourself. You can choose to be a Creator."*

"We've been sitting here 'creating' for days and nothing has happened! They are getting stronger and we are getting weaker!" the plump woman argues. She is standing right at the door now, her children huddled around her. The youngest begins to cry.

"Plant a seed and you won't see growth for a while," Rada says. "Doesn't mean it isn't happening. You have to hold your vision."

"But how do you know if anything is changing?" the girl in overalls asks. "And how do you love yourself if – if you've done terrible things?"

"They are the two hardest things in the world to do," Rada agrees. "Appearances are very convincing."

A bomb blasts outside and it is so deafeningly loud that everyone claps their hands to their ears. The shrill sound of a siren begins and it wails on and on, and Nathan is terribly afraid that it's all over now, that they will all die.

But suddenly the noise stopped and someone rolled against him heavily, muttering, "Sorry. Forgot to turn the alarm off. At least we don't have to get up..."

It was Brett. Sunshine was pouring into the room through the open window, and a whole non-school day stretched ahead of them.

Chapter 4

TRACKING OPTIONS

Nathan did not usually enjoy English classes. Unlike his father, he was not very good at writing and English assignments usually filled him with dread. Especially the 'creative writing' ones, when he had to make up a whole story from scratch.

But this time it was different. An idea had popped into his head out of nowhere about these two groups of people, the Creators and the Reactors, and this battle they were in, and the story was unfolding in front of his eyes almost like a movie. It was as if he was there.

He sat at his desk, writing steadily, while the classroom clock ticked its way toward the end of the lesson. He could hear Brett sighing and fidgeting behind him, and someone else kept bumping their seat against the ground, but all of those sounds formed a vague, distant background. Front of his mind was a little group of rebels, the Creators, who were hanging out in a secret hideaway while the dark and oppressive Reactor regime took over their city, brainwashing people with depressing messages that were broadcast every day. It was looking desperate for the rebels... Their leader was a tall, muscular warrior with an amazing set of skills, like sword-fighting and the ability to run with phenomenal speed and take these huge, gravity-defying leaps through the air... but his main thing was his calmness. While everyone and everything was falling to pieces around him, the leader stayed really calm. He had piercing blue eyes and when he spoke, people listened. They stopped rushing around like headless chooks, and listened. The only thing was that the Reactors were getting closer and more powerful. They'd homed in on the rebels' hideaway and were gradually surrounding it.

Nathan had written himself into a hole. He had no idea how to get his heroes out of their dilemma. He paused to gaze outside for a moment, but nothing came to him. When his teacher called an end to the class, a whole lot of people burst to their feet in relief, chattering and clattering, but he moved quietly, frowning a little as he gathered his stuff and pondered over his problem.

He daydreamed about it as he cycled home, where he found his dad sitting on the couch, wrapped in a blanket and reading a magazine. Seeing Nathan, he put it aside and asked how school was going. Nathan's father looked pale and a bit grey these days, but at least today he was sitting up and taking an interest.

On an impulse, Nathan told him about the story, and his father sat up a little more, and a bit of a shine came into his eyes. "Can I read it?" he asked.

Usually Nathan would have hedged, saying, 'It's not

very good,' to keep his father's expectations down, but this time he didn't think to say that. The story *was* good. He knew it. It had tumbled out of his mind as if it came from some place where it was already fully written. Except for the ending, the solution to the problem. That had him stumped. He sat with his arms wrapped around his knees, trying to nut it out while his father read.

"It's great." Nathan's dad put the pages down and looked at him in admiration. "Mate, you've written a corker. How are you going to finish it?"

"That's the problem," Nathan admitted, shifting from the couch seat to the armrest. "I'm stuck."

His father nodded thoughtfully. "You've got them pretty hemmed in there."

"Yeah."

They sat in silence for a moment.

"Magic? Can they... do some incantation? Wave a wand? Has anyone got a magical object they can use?"

Nathan shook his head. That didn't feel right. "If they were going to use magic, they would have done it by now."

"Good point." His father scratched his tousled head. "How about brute force? Can they just charge out of there like madmen and take the enemy on? You've heard how people can lift cars off babies when they're desperate? Maybe they summon some kind of extraordinary strength?"

Nathan considered this for a moment. "Nah. Even if they were amazingly strong, they couldn't win. There's too many of the Reactors. And anyway, the whole point is that they *don't* fight back because that makes the enemy stronger."

His father nodded again. "Okay... What about

cunning? Intelligence? You know those shows where the detective figures out the crime from all sorts of little clues that don't seem to be at all connected? Maybe the rebels find a chink in the enemy's armour?"

"Mm." Nathan liked this. "But what?" he asked, sliding back off the armrest into the seat.

"There's always luck," his father added. "A lucky co-incident. The best writers call on it."

Nathan made a face. That would be wimping out. He didn't want to write, 'Suddenly all the Reactors began to stagger and fall to the ground, as if they'd contracted a strange, fatal disease...' That was too easy. There was no dignity for his warrior-leader in a solution like that.

"Yep. You're right," his father agreed when he objected to the luck idea. "You've got a good instinct for this. So it needs to be some kind of brilliance. Some insight."

"Yeah."

His mother arrived home then and she was all dressed up as if she'd been in to work, which she hadn't done for a while because of looking after dad. She walked straight into the lounge room and they could see that she was steaming angry.

"What's up?" Nathan's dad asked, and she answered almost before the words were out of his mouth, tossing her bag onto a chair and stalking restlessly up and down the room.

"I've been retrenched. Can you believe it? Can you frigging believe that they would kick us when we're down? They know I'm here looking after you! What were they thinking?" Her arms shot out into the air in a furious, questioning gesture.

Nathan looked at his father anxiously. The old dark shadow was back; worry had wiped the shine out of his eyes. He was frowning, breathing heavily.

"God, sorry," Prue said. "Nathe, I didn't even see you there. Don't stress, mate, it's actually not such a bad thing." She lifted a knee and reached down to twist one of her crazy, high-heeled shoes off while the other ankle wobbled dangerously. "I need to be home with Dad right now, so this is a bit of a godsend in a way." The second shoe dropped off and she joined it on the carpet with a little bump. "Honestly. They've given me a pretty good package and I'll find work again easily when I need to. I've got the Midas touch in interviews." She grinned, stretching and wriggling her toes. "It's just that I'm mad at them for being so thoughtless. I mean, who sacks someone when they're down? Really!"

"We can always rely on Nathan to save us," Dad said unexpectedly. "He's writing a bestseller."

"A bestseller without an ending," Nathan corrected.

"It will come," his dad said encouragingly. He closed his eyes and the tired shadow swept over his face again.

Nathan glanced at his mother. She was watching the lumpy figure on the couch.

"Maybe it doesn't need an ending," she said after a moment. "Maybe it just finishes, leaving everyone hanging and you don't know what happens. I hate stories that end like that but lots of writers do it."

But that didn't feel right. This problem needed to be resolved. He couldn't just write 'The End' and leave them sitting there, about to be crushed by a superior force. He couldn't let his warrior-leader be defeated.

Nathan rolled the pages of his story together into a tube and looked through it at the TV, almost as if he hoped to find the answer written on its black screen. Nothing. He moved the cylinder a bit and his mother's face appeared in the little hole. She was looking at him and smiling sadly.

They are sitting in a tight circle on the floor and outside is dark and noisy. The enemy is right upon them. Rada is asking each person, one by one, about the thing they most regret, the thing they most reject about themselves. The girl in overalls won't say. She shakes her head. The mother has stayed in the room, reluctantly, fearfully, all of her children piled together in her broad lap like a litter of puppies. "No self-control," she confesses, shame-facedly. The thinnish man says, "Bad temper." A grey-haired man whispers, "I killed someone. By accident, but it happened. I've never been able to forgive myself." A dark and beautiful woman speaks mournfully in a strange accent: "I pushed him away. He loved me, but I pushed him away." An old woman murmurs, "I've wasted my life…"

Rada looks at Nathan questioningly. "I've stopped loving my dad," he says, and a hot flush rises through his body. The words land in the silence like heavy, black stones. They horrify him.

"What's yours?" the thinnish man asks Rada.

"Fear," she replies, with a half-smile. "Self-doubt."

The girl in overalls lifts her chin a bit. "I stole

from my sister," she says miserably. "I stole the thing she most cherished."

Outside, a pounding begins on the doors and walls of their mirrored room. Faces jerk to the periphery, eyes widen.

*"Yoohoo!" Rada sings out softly. "Their greatest weapon is our self-rejection," she reminds them, and gradually the faces turn back to the centre of the room, toward her. "Reactors take the form of whatever we hate in ourselves. They **want** us to react. They want us to judge ourselves."*

"But that's right! We've done bad things," the girl in overalls protests.

"Are you sure?" Rada asks.

"Of course," the dark woman exclaims. "We must beg forgiveness of those we have hurt."

"Phooey! Have you ever been inside the Reactors' Secret Room?"

"What secret room?" the others demand, alert.

"It's the place where they put all the ideas that don't fit their model." She hums quietly for a moment. "Like the Problem of Measurement."

"What problem of measurement?" asks the thinnish man.

"The fact that things don't exist until you measure them - or observe them."

The greyish-haired man murmurs, "Yes, I've heard that... Events are neutral and we give them meaning."

"Exactly. A problem is only a problem when you

call it that. It could be an opportunity. A blessing."

Something explodes outside and the blast reverberates the mirrored walls. Everyone jumps, expecting the glass to crack and shatter. It doesn't, but they shrink closer together, fearfully.

*"How is **this** an opportunity?" the dark woman mutters in her strange accent. "I followed you here because I do not believe in those Reactorss! But they grow stronger while we chat!"*

"They grow stronger while we resist them," Rada corrects. "While we interpret them as enemies." She looks at Nathan. "So, what endings have you considered? Magic, brute strength…"

"Cunning," he replies. "Luck. Just leaving it hanging. But none of them seems right."

"Because there's another option," she says. "And that's the Power of the Light."

"What light?" he asks.

A blue and red light is circling the walls of the room, making a noise that's painful to the ear. Feet are hurrying past, and he hears urgent voices. They are speaking in low tones but it's as if they're right next to him. A strange man's voice says, "This way, easy does it," and Nathan's eyes popped open in alarm.

He sat up in bed, heart racing, straining to hear.

Chapter 5

LOOKING IN THE MIRROR

They were taking his dad in an ambulance. Grandad and Grandma stood on the porch on either side of Nathan, and the three of them watched the ambulance pull away into the darkness with his parents.

"We'll visit in the morning," Grandma said soothingly, her arm tight around Nathan's shoulders. "He'll be fine."

Grandad's jaw was clamped shut and his fingers were digging into Nathan's hand. He seemed to realise, and let go. He and Grandma were wearing coats over their pyjamas.

"Who's for a cup of tea or hot milk?" Grandma asked cheerfully.

Grandad grunted, and the three of them walked slowly into the bright kitchen. It was three a.m. Grandma had been there so often lately she knew where everything was straight off. While she was making them drinks, Grandad's phone rang and they all jumped. You didn't expect anyone to ring at that hour of the night. It was Aunt Cherry. Grandad went into the lounge room to talk to her privately.

Nathan wondered if he really had stopped loving his dad. It was just that he wanted the pain to stop. He wanted the old happy days back. He pushed the image of his father on the stretcher out of his mind. He turned away from the memory of his mother's anxious face as she climbed into the ambulance. He wanted magic, brute force, brilliance, luck – anything except leaving it all hanging.

In the morning Cherry was there. She glanced briefly at the neat stack of health information books and magazines on the kitchen table, but said nothing. They drove into the hospital together. She sat in the back with Nathan, holding his hand and stroking it gently, but no one was saying anything. Grandad hadn't even remembered to put the car radio on.

Dad was still alive. It was funny but Nathan realised he'd been worrying all night that they'd arrive to the news that his dad was dead. Well, not funny; awful, really, to be wondering something like that. It was just that it was on everyone's mind. You could pick up the thought. It wafted from person to person like a bad smell.

His mother was sitting by his father's bedside. They both looked pale but at least everyone was alive.

That was a long day.

The whole day was like a game of musical chairs, with someone sitting in the seat next to the bed and someone standing at the foot of the bed and two or three someones taking turns out in the corridor or the visitors' room since they were only allowed so many people in Dad's room at a time. When it was Grandad's turn in the chair, Prue and Grandma went to the caf for a cup of tea. Nathan was lying on the floor playing a game on his phone; the men must have forgotten he was there.

"Pull yourself together, son," Grandad said harshly. "Your good wife is struggling. You can beat this thing!"

"You don't know what you're talking about," Nathan's father replied wearily. "It's got me."

"I didn't raise defeatists!" Grandad spat. "Face it! Conquer it, son!"

"Like you've conquered drink?" Nathan's father asked wryly. "Should I follow your example?"

"You've got no spirit of forgiveness," Grandad said bitterly.

"I grew up watching you push Mum around every time you got pissed! You think I've got any time for *your* opinions? You think I've got any respect for *you*?" Nathan's dad coughed noisily and with a rustle of the bedding, he turned away from his father.

After a few minutes, Nathan heard Grandad heave himself out of the chair and leave the room. Alone in the bed, his dad began to cry. It was a whimpery, moany sound that stopped as soon as Prue and Grandma returned. Nathan sat huddled on the floor, feeling sick.

"But what can I do to help?" Nathan asks.

*"Decide how **you** want it to go," Rada tells him. "Forget how it looks and Create the story **you** want to experience."*

"But that's not real."

"Phooey!" she says. "Real shmeal. Real is what you make it."

"So what's this 'power of the light', then?" he asks. "Is it like a laser sword or something?"

"It's the light of Truth and Understanding," Rada replies, "which is another kind of sword. It's Love too."

'Love' is not a word that Nathan can relate to. Particularly now. And he doesn't get how truth is going to save them. Or how it's like a sword.

Something heavy thuds against the wall outside, and the mirrors vibrate.

The big woman shudders and draws her children closer.

"Loving yourself transforms the enemy," Rada says. "It's that simple, folks. In fact, the enemy dissolves in front of your eyes when you own it, when you love your whole self, warts and all."

The heavy thing begins striking the wall with a steady, repetitive, booming thud. They are so clearly trapped now that no one even thinks of running anymore. They are sitting almost hopelessly, on the floor in a circle in this bare room with mirrored walls, while outside monsters and Reactors are closing in on them. And their leader is talking about love instead of arming them. How disappointing.

"But how do you love your evil side? How do you love your weakness?" Overall-Girl asks.

"Who says it's evil?" Rada challenges. "What if it's just as sacred as your good side? What if there's

no such thing as evil? What if it just looks that way because our seeing is crooked?"

They frown at her, wincing each time the thing pounds into the wall.

"And what if we transform it as soon as we see its purpose?" She leaps to her feet and drags the beautiful, dark-haired woman up. "You pushed him away – good! How was that the best thing you could possibly have done?"

The woman shakes her head in confusion.

Rada drives her toward the mirror. "Look. What do you see?"

"I see me. I'm afraid."

The glass vibrates and she takes a step back in horror.

"Now I see an evil woman – she is terribly beautiful but she is waiting to rip out my soul –"

Nathan and the others peer at the glass, trying to see what she is seeing.

*"Don't react," Rada says quietly. "**Think**. How was pushing him away the greatest gift you could give him?"*

"I gave him his freedom," the woman says unwillingly. "He found another, and he loves her. And she adores him." She stares defiantly at the evil woman no one else can see

"And you? How was that the best thing for you?"

The dark-haired woman has her back to them so they cannot see her face, but tears fill the eyes of her reflection. "I poured my soul into my art," she says.

"You made it mean loss and error but it was also freedom and joy and creativity and love."

"Yes."

As the word escapes her lips a light flashes out from within the woman and from within her reflection at the exact same moment. The two lights meet and merge. They see the fear and grief melt away from her face. She smiles. She laughs. And the next moment she walks straight through the mirror and is gone.

Rada turns to the rest of them. They are all staring, goggle-eyed. "Who's next?" she asks.

The grey-haired man speaks at once. "Me." He struggles to his feet.

*"Where have you **given** life?" Rada asks him.*

He frowns. "I'm a healer. I save lives. But I have also lost lives."

"Look in the mirror. What do you see?"

"Grief. Regret."

"Now think of those who died."

For some reason Nathan thinks of his father. He hears Rada ask, "You think you did it to them, but which part of them wanted to die?" And instead of the old man's reply, he hears his father saying, "It's better this way. I'm a waste of space. I'm screwing everything up."

Nathan opened his eyes in shock. He climbed out of bed and walked to the bathroom, switched on the light, and went to stand in front of the mirror. He stared into his eyes and saw his father there. And his mother. And Grandad and

Grandma and Nan and Pa.

"Smoke and mirrors," he murmured.

Chapter 6
THE SEED OF CHANGE

Nathan's father was back home from hospital but he was weak and depressed. He slept all day or just lay in bed staring at the wall. Prue alternated between red-eyed, weepy days when she could hardly stop crying, and angry days when she slammed doors and banged things down, and quiet moody days when she was so preoccupied that she hardly seemed to hear anything that Nathan said. And then she had her bright, positive, 'we can get through this' days, but there seemed to be fewer and fewer of those.

Grandad had stopped visiting. Grandma still came, with baskets full of food, looking worried and pretending to be cheerful for Nathan. He didn't know which was worse: everyone being depressed or everyone pretending cheerfulness.

It was one day when Cherry was there that things started to change. Nathan was in his room frowning over his story, which was supposed to be handed in the next day, when Cherry walked past his open door and went into her brother's room. It was quiet in there for a while but then she said, "The only time Dad stopped working was when we were really sick – it was the only way we could get the attention we needed."

Nathan was leaning across to bump his door shut when she added, "Do you think – no, listen: do you think you're trying to get his attention?"

There was a quiet moment, which would have been Nathan's dad mumbling something in reply, and then Cherry said in her strong, clear voice, "I know you've pushed him away. You're testing him and he won't be up for it. But Matt, this isn't about him. It's about you."

For a second time Nathan went to close his door and again Cherry's words stopped him. "Rubbish! You've got to get over that, Matthew. So he wasn't there for us! So he was a shit father! So what? You going to let your resentment of him kill you? You're being as unavailable right now to your son as Dad was to you – worse if you bloody go and die on him. Honestly and truly, there are things you could be doing to turn this around and you're lying here like a child feeling sorry for yourself!"

It was quiet again. Nathan looked at the last sentence he had written in his story: *'We will call upon the Power of the Light!" Rados, the Warrior-Leader declared.*

He frowned, thinking.

"I'm sorry." Cherry went on more gently: "That was cruel. Who am I to talk? You know, maybe this is also about being kinder to yourself. You've worked your guts out..." Her voice trailed away, and after a few moments Nathan realised he was straining to hear, and he gave up trying.

But also, a new sentence had come to him, and then another: *The Reactors were only seconds away but the Creators stopped looking at them. They stopped giving them any attention. Rados summoned them together in a circle and they linked hands and focused their minds on Freedom. As they did, a brilliant light began pouring out of their foreheads, as powerful as a laser. And then light started to beam out of their hearts and their eyes, and they could feel it vibrating through their hands...*

It is swirling, weaving in and out around each person like a shimmering stream, fascinatingly beautiful. Nathan feels as if the worries of years are lifting off him and melting away. He feels warm and safe, and his hands are tingling. The others are smiling – somehow Nathan knows that everyone is feeling this extraordinary sense of wellbeing and everyone's hands are tingling, even those of the people on the other side of the circle. It's as if he can feel what everyone is feeling all at once. And they're all in here, even the ones who had walked out through the mirror. Or maybe everyone has walked through the mirror...? That must be it because everyone is smiling, like they have some amazing secret, some invincibility. And everyone is glowing with this amazing light.

'It's love,' he thinks in surprise, and kind of in slow motion he notices that the first of the Reactors is upon them. Its face is contorted with fury and it starts

to shout, and odd words like 'Stupid!' and 'Hate you!' explode from its mouth and then pop and dissolve, like bubbles. Nathan sees the furious expression turn to confusion and then wonderment, and the Reactor's face softens and slowly fades, until it has disappeared altogether.

"What do you think?" Rada asks, in a thoughtful tone.

"It's awesome," Nathan enthuses. "Wow! I never knew Light could do that."

"Yes. The thing is, everything is made of Light. There's nothing that isn't."

Another Reactor reaches them and goes through the same furious shouting/confusion/ wonderment/ dissolving process, as if the energy of their circle is a force field of some kind. A magical, lucky, powerful, brilliant force field…

"Want to play a game?" Rada asks, her head cocked to one side, cheeky dimpled smile.

"Now?" he replies, surprised.

"Sure."

"Okay…"

"It goes like this: you pick something that you want to change. Might be big, might be small, but it has to matter to you. And then you imagine something really fun happening to make that true."

"Like what?"

"Like… say you've got ants in your pants and you want to get rid of them."

"Okay," he grins.

"So you imagine this great vacuum cleaner sucking them out of your pants! Or a queen ant coming along and saying, '**Atten-shun! All ants fall in!**' And they just march away. Boom-de-boom-de-boom."

"Does it really work?"

She shrugs. "Try it and see. We were created to Create, right?"

Suddenly there are Reactors on both sides of them. One is shouting at Rada and the other is shouting at him. He and Rada exchange glances and smiles, and she squeezes his hand.

"**Everything** is love," she says. "No matter how it looks. When you recognise that, you can transform anything."

She turns and looks right at that ugly Reactor and straight away it starts to sort of foam at the mouth and look confused and then it dissolves into the swirling light. And Nathan locks eyes with the Reactor on his side which is yelling, '**Mean! Unkind! Cruel! Scared! Angry!**' which are all his own thoughts, he realises, and he stops fighting them and just thinks, 'Yep'. And a very strange thing happens because he sees this movie of his dad being sick and all the people turning up to say how much they care and love him, and his Grandad and his dad facing up to each other, and his aunt Cherry being reunited with his dad, and his mum getting stronger, and his idea for the story, and his friend Brett being there for him, and his dad being proud of him, and his dad… his dad… being asked to choose, to not give up, to choose and to love… and *he sees his fear that he has stopped loving his father. How ridiculous. Of course he hasn't.*

And then his father is right there, above him, leaning blurrily over him.

"I'm not going anywhere," Nathan's father whispered, stroking his hair gently. "I'm not leaving you." There were tears in his eyes.

Chapter 7

THE GAME

A suitcase lay open on his bed and his mother was tossing clothes from his wardrobe into it.

"What's going on?" Nathan asked, halting in the doorway and dropping his schoolbag at his feet.

"We're going away," Prue said. "For a holiday."

"Now? It's term-time."

"Do you mind?" She stopped turfing his clothes and looked at him.

Nathan shrugged. "How long for?"

"Two weeks. To the beach house."

"Oh..." He wandered in and sat on the bed. "Is Dad coming too?"

"Yep." A bunch of his t-shirts sailed past and landed in the open case.

Some holiday this would be, Nathan thought. Nothing like taking miserableness to your favourite place...

"When are we going?"

"Tonight."

"What about school?"

"It's all sorted." She squatted and dragged some shoes out of the tangled mess at the bottom of his wardrobe. "I know you'll miss out on seeing your friends, but... Dad's more important right now. We've got to turn him around."

"I know," Nathan said. He pulled a green long-sleeved shirt out of the case. "Not this one. I hate it."

It was off-season so the frenetic seaside town that he'd only known at the height of summer was quiet as anything. There were no hordes of people on the beach or in the parks, and the cafés and restaurants that were always crowded in his memory were empty, or closed... Nathan's favourite ice cream parlour was closed. He hovered outside it when they were going for a walk along the quiet, main road. It was dark inside and the seats were upside down on the tables. The 'three-flavours special' sign was leaning against a wall.

"Oh well," Prue said. "It's not really ice cream weather anyway." She came up close behind him and said quietly, "I'm reading one of Cherry's books. It's very anti-sugar – especially for... what Dad's got. I'm going to cut it right out for a while and see if that helps. Will you go along?"

"Okay," Nathan sighed. Her reflection in the glass smiled at him and ruffled his hair. Behind her, the street was damp and empty, reflecting a wishy-washy grey sky. His father sat, bulky in his winter coat, on a street bench, gazing at some squabbling seagulls.

Prue was stir-frying vegies for dinner. They could hear the sizzle and snap from the kitchen. Nathan lay on the floor playing games on his phone. His father sat on the couch, eyes closed.

"Did you ever finish that story?" his father asked suddenly.

"Yeah."

"Brilliance?"

"Light," Nathan said. He'd almost forgotten about the story. He'd handed it in the very day they'd left for this holiday.

Matt cocked his head. "Light?"

"Power of the Light."

"Power of the light," his father echoed. "I'm intrigued. Tell me more."

"Kind of a laser light." Nathan put the phone down on the carpet beside him and stretched. He lifted his chin, dragging the back of his head against the floor, and his gaze gathered up his upside-down father. "They get together in a circle and everyone holds hands and imagines this really powerful light coming out of their foreheads and chests, and when the Reactors turn up, they just kind of... melt away..."

"Oh. I thought you didn't want a magic solution."

Nathan frowned. He rolled over and sat up. "You know when we saw *Avatar* and you were disappointed in the ending? You said it's crazy that a superior, more evolved race reacts to the warring Americans at their same level. You said it would have made more sense if they acted out their own powers – if they sat at their Home Tree and used the power of their minds to turn the army away."

"Yes..." his father agreed.

"So that's what my characters were doing. Power of the mind."

"But you called it light."

"'Cause that's how mind power looks. Instead of putting their energy into fighting evil, they're using their minds to create what they want. Which I s'pose is a kind of magic," he added thoughtfully.

His father nodded slowly. "And a kind of brilliance. Sounds good. I'd like to read it. Got it here?"

"I handed it in."

"Damn," Prue exclaimed in the kitchen. She poked her head around the door. "I forgot the soy sauce – would you believe it?"

"Shoot you at dawn," Nathan's dad said automatically. "You'd better farewell your loved ones."

She stuck her tongue out at him. "It's ready. Two min."

"Have you ever thought of... using your mind to get rid...?" Nathan asked.

"Of the tumour? No."

"Why don't you?"

"Seems pretty airy-fairy to me."

"I think you should try."

"What, just imagine it getting up and walking away?"

"No, Dad!" Nathan scoffed, and then he said, "Well, I s'pose you could. Or you could imagine this super-powerful vacuum cleaner sssssucking it out of you. Or a SWOT team going in and *bombing* it out of you!"

His father made a face. "I've had enough violence already."

"Okay. Then a magician just reaching in and taking it out or turning it into a butterfly that flies away. Or you could use the Power of the Light," Nathan challenged, narrowing his eyes, "and imagine a brilliant laser light changing that part of you back to normal."

"Dinner!" Prue called.

"Well, if it worked for your characters," his dad said, heaving himself off the couch.

Cherry's book was propped open on the table with a tomato sauce bottle. Matt sighed when he saw it.

"Don't," Prue warned, handing him a plate of stir-fry. "It's actually pretty compelling. I think it's worth a try. At least do it for your sister, if not for yourself."

"I've flicked through it," he said. "It's anecdotal stuff – no studies, no medical proof."

"We've tried the medical model," she said, serving Nathan, "and it made you sick as a dog. Some of these stories... well, they're pretty inspiring. And if it's possible for those people..."

Matt sighed again. "Between the two of you..." he said, jerking his head in Nathan's direction.

Prue's face was a question.

"Nathe wants me to use my mind to get rid of it."

"Well, why not?" she said, taking a forkful. "Let's go over to the other side for a while."

"The dark side?" Matt asked, jokingly.

"No," Nathan said, "the light side."

He stopped in the doorway of his parents' bedroom, on his

way to bed. "Have you tried it?"

Matt looked at him from amongst a nest of pillows. "Tried what?"

"You know. Power of the Light. Imagining it gone."

"Not yet."

"Do it now." Nathan came and sat on the side of his father's bed. "Go on."

"I can't figure out if I'm going to use the giant vacuum cleaner or the laser light," Matt said seriously. A welcome touch of his old, dry humour.

"Or it could be our rubbish removal guys," Nathan replied, equally serious. "You could imagine them coming in with their noisy old truck, waking up all your other organs with their clattering, and getting that stupid old lump. Or it could be like the witch in *The Wizard of Oz* who dissolves when you throw water all over her – maybe the lump just sizzles and fizzles out when you throw water on it. Or maybe it's got its own kind of kryptonite and you can blast it with something that makes it go weak and wither away."

"It strikes me," his father said after a moment, "that the word 'imagine' is made of 'I' and 'mage'. You know what 'mage' means, don't you?"

"Magician." Nathan smiled.

Chapter 8

THE MAGE AT WORK

Nathan's father did not put any store by this imaginary stuff, but he felt better after they did that visualisation. It was probably just the feeling of being active, of doing something about it instead of lying there passively. Whatever it was, he agreed to do it again in the morning, and at odd times through the day when Nathan saw him with his eyes closed, or with a faraway expression, it turned out that he was doing it again.

"I'm probably just imagining it," he said, "but I get a kind of warm, tingly feeling when I do it – some of the time." And he had his hand over the area of the tumour when he said that.

"I, mage," Nathan told him with a pointed finger. "I mean *you*, mage."

"You mage too," Matt replied with a little smile.

Prue had her nose in Cherry's book. "This guy reckons that you can turn genes on and off with your thoughts," she said. "I always thought our DNA controls us but he reckons it doesn't; *we* control *it*."

"Sick," Nathan enthused.

She looked at him over the book. "That really is the worst expression I have ever heard."

"We sure are going over to the dark side," Matt said.

"The *light* side," Nathan corrected. "If you resist something, you make it worse, but if you just ignore the yuck thing and I-mage it how you want it..."

"Ain't that the truth," Prue agreed. "Any kind of pain – you tense up and it's much worse. Arguments – definitely. This book even reckons that the whole cancer thing has become an epidemic since people 'declared war' on cancer."

"What were they supposed to do?" Nathan's father asked with a touch of irritation. "Lie down and surrender?"

"Learn from it. Take the message. Make lifestyle changes instead of attacking the cancer like it's the enemy."

"Then what is it?"

"A sign. A symptom that you're toxic."

"Thanks."

She bobbed her head. "You're welcome."

After lunch they went to the beach. It was deserted and cold when they got out of the car. Grey, washed-out skies met the grey sea in a long sweep from left to right.

They crunched down the concrete steps onto sand that was packed tight and hard. Prue took their hands, one on each side, and they walked in silence.

Nathan's thoughts went to Brett, and school, and wondering what was happening over there in his everyday life. It all seemed so far away. School was your whole life when you were a kid. From the time you were little and everyone talked about going to 'big school', and got you all excited about it, and then you went and it was okay but such a pain to have to go every single day, whether you felt like it or not. And then you went to high school and it was still a pain to have to go every single day. And then, he supposed, you became an adult and work was like that – you had to go every day whether you felt like it or not. There was something crazy about a world where everybody followed someone else's system like they were cogs in a machine.

Walking here on the beach with the steady lapping of waves and the smell of salt, and the quietness, the stillness, he wondered about what was real. *This* felt real, but maybe that was just because he was here now. Did classrooms and whiteboards and school bells seem as real when he was there? Was homework real? He thought about movies and advertising and peak hour traffic and supermarkets and computers. It all had to be real but none of it felt as real as a tree does when you lean up against it. Or as real as this beach and that sea. Maybe the earth was the real stuff and everything else was a dream made up by humans; a very busy dream that goes faster and faster until something happens to stop it all and pull you out of it. Like it had with his dad, who had slowed down, like an old tree, as if he was getting back to being real...

It began to drizzle, so they turned back to the car, and as they drove home it really set in. It rained steadily for their last three days at the beach house, and the rainbow that arced over the rooftops of houses as they were preparing to leave was truly beautiful.

On the front doorstep of their house Prue grabbed her husband's sleeve.

"What?" Matt asked, hand frozen at the lock.

"The house won't have changed. Don't walk back into it."

"You want us to live out here, on the porch?"

"*No,* silly." She squeezed his arm and Nathan's shoulder at the same time. "Don't walk back into the old habits. We've made some changes. Let's keep going – don't let the old ways drag us down."

A little muscle twitched in Matt's jaw but he said nothing; just gave a little nod, and they walked into the silent, dark house.

"I'm going to open all the windows," Prue said loudly, "and air this place out. It stinks in here."

So they had to pile on extra jumpers for a few hours while a freezing wind coursed through the place. Nathan's father muttered from under blankets on the couch, and Nathan shivered in front of the computer, but crazy as it was to have everything open in the middle of winter, the house felt better when they finally closed up and put the heater on.

"What's your mother up to now?" Matt asked with a head cocked towards the kitchen after yet another thud. "Go check, would you?"

Prue was standing inside the pantry with the rubbish bin at her feet and a packet in her hands. She was reading the ingredients on the label. She gave a little shake of her head and dropped the packet into the bin.

"What are you doing?" Nathan exclaimed. "They're my barbeque shapes!"

"Not any more, mate. I'm cleaning out.

"Yeah but not food we can *eat*. That's a waste."

"It was full of crap. I can't believe how much of this stuff is rubbish. Do you know the tuna had sugar and flavourings and *milk products* in it? I thought it was plain fish!"

"So?"

"So we're cleaning up. Can't expect Dad to be clean on the inside if we're putting this crap into him."

"*I'm* not sick," Nathan protested, catching sight of packets of chips and instant noodles in the bin.

Prue looked at him. "Now, maybe, but it catches up with you. My god." She gave a little giggle. "How am I going to look Cherry in the eyes?"

"She'll be happy," Nathan said grudgingly.

"I know. Oh well, I'll get over it."

"So what are we going to eat?" Nathan asked. "You're getting rid of everything."

"Fruit and veg mostly. Food that's alive."

He made a face, and just at that moment there was a knock on the kitchen door and Mrs O appeared in the window. She beamed and waved.

"Oh, crumbs," Prue said.

Nathan opened the door and their neighbour stepped in, sausage-like in a tightly-zipped parka, with a cake tin hugged to her chest.

"Just a little welcome-back treat," she beamed. "Did you have a nice holiday? Everything was fine here. I've got your mail in this plastic – oh!"

"Thanks, June," Prue said, catching the cake tin just in time. "You're very kind. It's just that..."

"Goodness... Did things go off while you were away?" Their neighbour's gaze was riveted to the overflowing rubbish bin.

"Not exactly," Prue hedged. "I'm researching a different diet for Matt... we're cutting out all processed food."

"Processed food!" Mrs O echoed. "What's that?"

Nathan looked at his mother.

"Well... anything that's not raw, I guess," she said. "We're going to keep to a very simple diet for a while."

"Fancy!" Mrs O breathed, raising her brows. "You won't be wanting this then," indicating the cake tin. "*It's processed.*"

"Perhaps we can have one last treat!" Prue declared in a rush. "We do love your cakes..."

"How is he then, the poor love?" their neighbour asked, looking past them toward the living room.

"All right. Not too bad at all," Prue said. "And how's Jack? And yourself?"

"Oh, all's well with us. Jack's complaining about his back, but that's nothing new. And my arthritis is worse. We're not getting any younger!" She looked around the kitchen, her gaze hovering over the rubbish bin again. Nathan was eyeing it a bit covetously too. Maybe, when his mother wasn't looking, he'd pull out that bag of chocolate chip cookies...

When Mrs O had finally left, Prue went back to emptying the pantry and Nathan sat on the table and watched.

"Shouldn't we at least give this stuff to someone?" he asked at last. "Like Mrs O – or poor people. Someone."

His mother looked stricken. "Oh! Nathe! That's what I could have done. I wasn't thinking... It's too late now. I can't exactly give her stuff that she's seen in our bin, even though a lot of the packets are sealed..." Prue lifted a pack of ginger snap bickies out of the rubbish and turned it around in her hand. There was a clump of dust clinging to it. She brushed the dust off, looked at Nathan, and then dropped it back into the bin.

He groaned dramatically and clutched his chest. "I can't bear to see such waste of sugar... It's cruel."

Prue looked at him with narrowed eyes. She lifted some biscuits back out and began to read the ingredients. "Glucose, invert sugar, *three* numbers... Sound like real food to you?"

"Maybe it's getting us ready for the food of the future – you know, when real food has run out and we just swallow tablets."

His mother made a face. "That's a future I'm not in a hurry to reach."

"No cooking, no dentists," Nathan enticed. "I thought you hated cooking and dentists."

"Ah!" Prue batted him gently on the side of his head. "I don't hate cooking. I hate cooking when I'm not inspired or I'm rushing or no one likes what I've cooked. But I'm reinspired now, mate. I'm discovering all sorts of vegetable dishes that look fabulous that I can't wait to try – and an intriguing raw dessert thingo made out of dates and almonds and cashews and coconut and cocoa nibs, whatever they are, that I'm going to make today. As soon as I've been shopping. I'm going to repopulate this pantry with good, wholesome, life-giving food." She held Mrs O's glad-wrapped cake over the bin. "Going..."

"I thought you said we'd eat this last one!"

"I was lying. Going..."

Nathan's gaze was riveted to the dangling cake. After all the times his mother had told him not to waste food...

Prue hesitated. "It's mostly white flour and white sugar. There's really nothing very healthy in here. If we don't draw the line now, when will we?"

"I'm not stopping you!" he said, irritated, clasping his arms around his legs as if to prevent himself from leaping to the rescue of the poisonous cake.

It dropped into the bin with a resounding thud; the bin wobbled.

"What's going on in there?" Dad called from the lounge. "And what's for dinner? I'm hungry!"

Prue yanked the plastic bag full of rubbish out of the bin and tied a knot in it. "Just going shopping!" she called back. "We've got Mother Hubbard's cupboard."

Nathan rolled his eyes.

"You sure?" Dad's voice came again, full of doubt. "I thought there was heaps in it..."

"Yep," Prue said firmly. She grabbed her shoulder bag and headed rapidly out the back door, which banged behind her. A moment later Nathan heard the lid of the big green garbage bin outside thudding shut, and then the gate. He sat there on the kitchen table, swinging his legs, considering his options...

Chapter 9

THE TEST

Nathan stands alone in a field. It is very quiet. He turns slowly in a circle, but all directions reveal the same view: a hilly expanse of grass and trees and cloudy sky. Perhaps there is someone or something happening over the hill nearest to him? He takes the narrow path that weaves its way up the hillside through the waving grass, a frown puckering his forehead. Where is everyone? Where is Rada? Where is the war? Where are the Reactors? Has everyone been killed? Or have the Reactors all dissolved into bubbles and, if they have, where are the people?

It's quite hot. He pushes his sleeves up and plods further up the hill, hoping for a good view of the other side, and some sort of clue. The hill is deceptively steep. Rada is right: it takes much more energy going up than down. He is almost at the summit when he senses a shudder beneath his feet. He stops in alarm. Did the earth move?

He stamps cautiously. Nothing. The ground feels solid. Once again, all is still and quiet. It is quite disconcerting. He plods on, beginning to feel anxious.

There is a tree on the summit of the hill; it provides a satisfying destination. When he reaches it, Nathan surveys the landscape on all sides and is troubled by the same emptiness. No one and nothing to be seen: just that unbroken grassy ocean.

His only company is this tree, this gnarled old tree that stands here alone, leafy branches outstretched in all directions, trunk of average thickness, roots protruding from the ground. Sitting among the roots, he rests back against the trunk and closes his eyes. The tree feels solid behind him, as if it has been here forever and always will. This tree would not react to anything, he reflects. It just is.

All at once he feels it again: a shudder beneath the surface of the ground. He sits up, alert, hands gripping the roots on either side of him. To his amazement, a patch of grass just ahead of him suddenly shakes and lifts. Nathan leaps to his feet in alarm. A neat square of grass is laid aside and a head appears. It's the thinnish man. His face is as bloody and gashed and dirty as before. He shades his eyes against the sunlight and beckons to Nathan.

"Come on! We've gone underground."

"Why?" Nathan asks. "And who?"

"All of us! To hide, of course, from the Reactors," the man says, as if speaking the most obvious truth in the world.

"But…" Nathan gestures around him. "There aren't any!"

"Of course there are!" the man retorts. "Come on, hurry!"

"But where are they?" Nathan asks, approaching him uncertainly.

"Later, later. We've got to get you into hiding first!" the man says urgently. "Quick, down here."

With a last glance around the peaceful scene, Nathan puts his feet into the hole and drops into it after the thinnish man, who has disappeared from sight. He lands, squatting, and can just see the legs and feet of the man crawling away from him down a dark, narrow tunnel. Nathan follows, creeping and wriggling for what seems like a very long distance through the confined space, only catching up with him when their descent levels out. They crawl out of the tunnel into a large cavern, and stand up, brushing the dirt from their clothes. It takes a while for Nathan's eyes to adjust to the dark, but gradually he makes out a crowd of people, all pressed together and listening to a man who is speaking intently, fist raised.

"We will resist!" he declares earnestly.

"Resist!" the people echo.

"We will never give in!"

"Never!"

"We will fight this darkness even if it takes every

last one of us!"

"Fight to the end!"

"Where's Rada?" Nathan asks the thinnish man at his side.

"Who? Oh, **her**. I don't know. Ssh, listen. This is our leader."

"I thought Rada was our leader."

"Not anymore. She disappeared on us. Some leader."

"She wouldn't do that," Nathan said, troubled.

"Well, can you see her?" the thinnish man asks defiantly, jerking his hand around the cavern.

Nathan cannot. He frowns.

"Now **sh!** Listen. Come closer."

Nathan approaches the crowd reluctantly. The leader person has turned from the crowd to the wall. There is a big screen hanging there. He points a remote at it and immediately a dark-haired man appears on screen. "The time for dreaming is over!" he shouts. "You must believe the evidence of your senses. The enemy grows stronger all the time. If you've been told by someone to Create What You Want, you are becoming part of the problem. YOU are the enemy! There is no Create-What-You-Want! That is a dream world for children. Stand up and join the adults. **Be responsible**. Fight the dark forces. Fight and resist, and you will overcome."

The crowd cheers and then breaks into conversation, everyone speaking at once and moving around. In the chaos, Nathan catches sight of the large woman with her brood of children.

He grabs the arm of the thinnish man. "But where are the Reactors?"

The man glares at him. "Out there, of course!" he barks, pointing wildly in several directions.

"You mean down here? With us?"

"Of course. Where else would they be?"

"Then why…?" **Why did we come down here?** Nathan wonders numbly, as the man darts away. The quiet, still countryside above them flashes into his mind.

He elbows his way through the crowd to the large woman. "Excuse me. Do you know where Rada is?"

"Rada?" She looks at him anxiously. "No. Do you?"

"No…"

They stare at each other.

"One minute we were all together and those Reactors were dissolving," Nathan frowns, "and the next minute Rada has disappeared and you guys are all here with him," pointing at the thinnish man, "and him," at the new leader. "I don't get it."

"I was torn," the woman confesses, seizing his arm, "between going with her and going with him. It's the children, you see, I have to do the right thing by them! I was so confused, and the next minute she was gone – and doesn't it make more sense to fight evil or even run from it than to… to just imagine that everything is as you want?"

"I don't know," Nathan says honestly. "That seems to make sense but it's true that when you fight something it gets stronger." He leans against her broad arm suddenly, pushing hard. She starts, and immediately resists him, pushing back and exclaiming, "What are you doing? Are you crazy!"

Nathan leans in even harder and she leans back against him, until they are both puffing. Her children tug at her skirts, wide-eyed and fearful, and a small crowd gathers.

"You see!" Nathan declares, stopping so suddenly that she takes a few involuntary steps forward and nearly bowls him over. "When you push against me you get stronger and more forceful. And we get more locked together."

"Are you saying we should surrender? Just give in?"

"That or just walk away," the thinnish man mocks. "Like someone else used to."

"No she wasn't," a voice calls. The girl in overalls emerges from the crowd. "And I bet she's in the Reactors' Secret Room."

"What room?"

"The one where they put the Problem of Measurement." The girl looks at the thinnish man boldly. A titter runs through the people gathering around them.

"There is no such room!" he blusters. "It's a figment of her imagination!"

"Like everything else," she grins.

Smoke and mirrors, Nathan remembers. He turns to the girl, "Hey! What do you want to Create?"

Her grin broadens even further. "Hm… Life back in the sunshine, doing something I love, and friends with my sister again."

"Okay, go to it!" he says, and he waves his hand as if brandishing a wand.

"What about you?" she beams.

"Home with Dad, helping him to get healthy again."

She waves an imaginary wand. "Go to it!"

The leader man appears. "What's going on here?" he asks the thinnish man.

"These people… I'm afraid they're part of the problem," the thinnish man says gravely.

"They're trying to Create What They Want!" someone yells from the crowd.

"Danger! The Enemy!" other voices cry out.

"Tell me, who here is Reacting right now?" Nathan demands, but they cannot seem to hear him or understand his question. The girl in overalls does. She reaches out her hand for his and smiles.

*"She **can't** be here, can she?" the girl says to Nathan. "Because if you hold focus, you're not doubting. You're not Reacting. Right?"*

"Right," he agrees, light dawning.

Around them, people are jostling and arguing, their voices rising in anxiety.

"Shall we go up?" she asks.

"Yes, let's."

They turn toward the tunnel, and the others are so busy arguing that they don't even see them walk away. The noise dies out behind them as they reach the squishy, narrow part where they have to get down on hands and knees. Nathan crawls forward in the darkness until he reaches the place where he can stand up again. He looks around for the sky, for light, but it's still dark everywhere.

Putting out his hand, he feels a hard, flat surface. He slides his hand around, searching, and finds a bumpy thing, like a switch.

As light flooded the kitchen, he contemplated his next step.

Chapter 10

THE BATTLEGROUND

He had been planning to get those choc chip cookies. That had been his last thought before dropping off to sleep. A midnight snack before all those yummy foods disappeared forever. And if he had them at midnight, he wouldn't disturb his father's new diet, and if his mother didn't know, it couldn't bother her, right?

But standing here in the glaring kitchen light, the remnants of his dream still curling around his mind, Nathan couldn't help feeling a little strand of discomfort. Sure, they couldn't see him, but *he* could see him. He would always know. And if he couldn't resist one little packet of bickies, how could he expect his dad to be a Mage and heal himself?

Nathan switched off the light and turned back towards his bedroom, but as he walked along the darkened hallway, eyes adjusting again, he heard a thud and a low moan. The sounds were coming from his father's office, which had been closed for weeks now.

He hesitated. Were they being robbed? Quietly,

warily, he approached. Yes, there was a line of light showing at the base of the door and definite sounds of movement within. Drawers were being opened and closed, something was making periodic thudding noises, and his father's chair was rolling creakily across the floorboards. That couldn't be a thief, surely? A muttered exclamation convinced him. He opened the door cautiously, and his dressing-gowned father looked up from a chaotic scene of paperwork in surprise.

"Nathe! What are you doing up?"

"What are *you* doing up? Are you working... in the middle of the night...?" He gazed at the piles all over his father's desk and floor.

"I'm not working," Matt said darkly. "I'm cleaning up. I couldn't sleep so I thought I'd catch up on some filing..." A shadow crossed his face as he glanced at the open filing cabinet and the stacks of paper on the floor and on his desk.

"Looks like you're going to be here for ages," Nathan observed.

His father frowned. "It's a disaster zone, isn't it?"

"Do you want some help?"

"Thanks, mate, but there really isn't anything you can do."

"I can keep you company," Nathan said.

His father looked at him properly for the first time. "You can't sleep either?"

Nathan shrugged. He wasn't quite ready to reveal that brush with his conscience. And besides, if his father knew the bin was full of chucked-out food, he might try to rescue it...

"Best you go back to bed," Matt said. "I appreciate your offer but there's no point both of us having a sleepless night, and I'll concentrate better if you're not here."

"Okay." He stood there for a moment, then said suddenly: "Actually a dream woke me up. You know that Reactors story? It came from some dreams. I thought they'd finished but I just had another one."

Matt surveyed him with interest. "Dreams, eh? A lot of great writers get their ideas from dreams."

"Really?"

"Yeah. And inventors too. So is the war over?"

Nathan shook his head. "Nope."

"That's a pity."

"Not really."

Matt cocked his head. "Why so?"

"Because it's this ongoing test." Nathan lifted a pile of folders off the spare chair, plonked them on the floor, and sat down. "I mean, the war is only there for the people who keep creating it – the Reactors, in this case, and anyone who reacts to *them*. That's because you become a Reactor by reacting – of course. But anyone who doesn't want to play that game can just opt out."

"I see." His father nodded thoughtfully, and then began to look again at the mess around him.

"Well, not just opt out," Nathan explained. "You've got to choose another game, something you want to create in your life. And then you get focused on that, and the other stuff disappears."

"Nice," Matt said distractedly. "Listen, mate, scoot off to bed and let me finish this. I'm behind in my filing by months and I don't want to leave Mum with –" He stopped, caught.

"What do you mean, 'leave mum with'?" Nathan asked into the midnight silence.

"With all the responsibility of supporting us," his dad replied, avoiding his eye, but Nathan was sure that wasn't what he had been about to say.

"You told me you weren't going to die," Nathan said, and the silence deepened.

"Of course not!" his father exclaimed, and then, curiously, "When did I say that?"

Nathan frowned in thought. He had a clear memory of his father leaning over him... but he couldn't recall...

"It doesn't matter. I'm not planning on dying, Nathan, it's just that I don't know what's going to happen. Hell, no one knows! Look at me now – no one knew this was around the corner. God, I'm sorry. I shouldn't even be having this conversation with you. I don't want you to worry..."

"I get more worried when there are secrets," Nathan said abruptly. "If you died, I'd have to grow up more, so you might as well treat me more grown-up now."

Matt looked at him strangely. His hand rose to cover his mouth, thumb and fingertips pressing deeply into his cheeks, as if he was preventing himself from speaking. His gaze locked with Nathan's. Then, taking a big deep breath, Matt drew his hand slowly away from his face, closing it in a fist in front of his lips for a few moments before letting it drop back into his lap.

"All right. You want a talk, man-to-man?"

Nathan gave a short nod, mouth dry.

"How old are you, Nathe? Remind me."

"Thirteen."

His father nodded slowly. He took a deep breath. He turned in his rotating office chair and looked at the mess around the room, and then he revolved back to face Nathan.

"I hope you do write, mate, because you've got potential. And I hope you find a way to beat the system, or at least make it work for you." He scratched his chin, sighed, and sat up in the chair. "If I'm going to be honest with you, you'll have to cope with a bit of a wake-up about your old Dad."

"Okay," Nathan said, sitting up also.

"Kids start off thinking their parents are perfect," his father said. "They seem to be all-knowing and all-powerful and super-wonderful when you're little, but as you get older, you realise they're not."

"Like when you don't keep your promises about going to the footy?"

Matt shook his head in embarrassment. "Yeah."

"Or like when you keep telling Mum you're going to fix the deck and build a shed and make a vegie garden, but you don't do any of it, and in the end she hires people?"

"All right, all right, don't rub it in!" His father gave a regretful smile. "I can see that I've fallen off your pedestal already. But what I'm about to tell you... I'll be lucky if you've still got any respect for me after this."

"Okay," Nathan said evenly, but his stomach felt tense and his hands were balled up in his lap, fingernails digging in.

Matt sat for a moment, thinking, drumming his fingers on the desktop. Then he turned to Nathan. "These last few years the publishing industry has been changing.

A lot. There are heaps more people writing now because it's so easy to get self-published – so that means a lot more competition. Book sales are down because of e-publishing, and traditional publishers are more picky than ever. In theory this means it's a level playing field – it's much easier for anyone to get their work out there. But it's harder to make money because there's such a glut of material that editors can pick and choose from, and often they're not paying for articles anymore. It's harder than ever to just be a writer; everyone has to market themselves if they want to get seen, and that's never been my forté. The last few years," he sighed heavily. "The last few years Mum's salary has been carrying us. I've hardly made a cracker. I didn't like how the industry was going so I pretty much turned a blind eye to it and waited for things to come good. Only they haven't."

The clock on his desk made the little clicking sound that indicated a new hour. They both looked at it automatically: two a.m.

Nathan's father shook his head, running his fingers through his hair. "This is crazy... You woke up from a dream and walked into a nightmare, eh?"

Nathan frowned. "I didn't know you weren't working much. You always seemed pretty busy."

"Yeah, busy doing nothing. I was stuffing around, mate. I was writing plenty but I wasn't sticking with any of my ideas long enough to make any decent money. You think that if you don't look at something it will go away or sort itself out, but too often it doesn't." He shook his head ruefully. "Sorry. It's no treat discovering your parents' shortcomings, is it?"

Nathan shrugged. "I guess I always sort of knew. I knew something wasn't okay but I didn't know what and I didn't want to look at it either. It was more fun watching TV."

They sat gazing at each other, and then both smiled.

"They say kids know more than we think," Matt said. "Mum always reckoned you looked wise, right from the day you were born." He glanced around again. "So that's it. I've been digging my head in the sand of my own stubbornness. Not going with the times. Determined to just write and ignoring the marketing side of things, and turning into a dinosaur in the process. It's as if Life was getting ready to kick me out since I wasn't carrying my own weight anymore – is this all too much for you?"

Nathan shook his head.

"I'm not blaming Life," his father added. "I was getting chewed up with guilt and stress over everything, and resenting Prue for bringing in the dough because I thought that should be my job, but at the same time not getting on with it and feeling ashamed about that. I reckon the cancer was my way of giving up without looking like a coward. It gave me a way to bow out with dignity... Or so I was thinking, in my darkest moments, until you started with that 'Mage' talk, and Mum started reading Cherry's books, and this idea got into me that maybe I didn't have to die after all."

"You don't," Nathan said at once.

"But tonight," his father ploughed on, "I couldn't seem to control my thoughts at all. I couldn't sleep. I was plagued with doubts and fears so I figured I'd get out of bed and do some catching up in here, and I came face-to-face with the god-almighty mess I've made in my business: I haven't chased debtors, I haven't followed up on pitches or ideas; I've got research and paperwork all over the frigging place!" As he said the last, he smacked the pile on the desk in front of him and scowled. "I know this isn't the done thing – dumping on your kid. You'd better think of it as an initiation rite into manhood: instead of having a tooth pulled out or having to trap a lion by yourself, you're having to face your old man's faults and flaws."

"It's probably easier to have a tooth pulled out," Nathan said seriously.

Matt laughed. He leaned across the gap between them and cuffed the side of Nathan's head. "Thanks."

Nathan twirled the office seat he was sitting on all the way around. "If you made the stress that made you sick, you can unmake it too."

"Yeah. In theory. Until I look at the size of the disaster I've created. That brings it all home. How out of control I've let things get. How out of control *I've* become." He stopped suddenly, staring at his son.

"What?" Nathan asked.

"I don't know. It just struck me..."

"What struck you?"

"How out of control I've become," his father repeated slowly.

Nathan watched him, a querying frown pulling at his forehead. Matt was frowning too, his eyes glazed with distant thoughts. After a while, Nathan spun the chair again, making it squeak on purpose.

"Can you cope with more?" his father asked, raising

his head and looking at him.

"I don't know. Is it bad?"

"I guess you've noticed that Grandad and I don't get on."

"It's crossed my mind."

"Smart arse." Matt smiled briefly. "What have I told you about it?"

"That he used to drink a lot. He still does – I've seen him."

"Yeah. But it used to be a helluva lot worse. He – don't let Grandma know you know this, Nathe. Keep it between us, okay?"

"Okay," Nathan breathed.

"He used to get pretty rough with Grandma, too. He never outright hit her, but he'd be rough and rude. I tried to stop him when I was little and he'd lash out at me and then be even more cutting toward Grandma, so I stopped... until I was big enough to stand up to him properly."

"But why did Grandma let him?" Nathan asked.

"Oh... who understands these things? She said he loved her, he wasn't a bad man, just couldn't handle the drink, and she had plenty of her own flaws so who was she to judge...? That's all very well but I couldn't stand it. I very nearly punched him, Nathe. I had him up against the wall one day, his collar bunched in my fist so tight he could hardly breathe... I don't know what kept me from killing him, I was so mad. After that he stopped being so aggressive but by then I'd lost all respect for him. I thought, what a cowardly, out-of-control son-of-a..." Matt shook his head slowly. "So all my life I've been angry with Grandad for being out of control of his drinking. And now I'm waking up to how out of control *I've* been..."

"The mirror," Nathan murmured.

"I read about this in an article once," Matt said thoughtfully. "The idea that anything that upsets you is a reflection of something in you, but you don't recognise the reflection because it shows up in another form. What did you say?"

"The mirror."

"What mirror?"

"What you said. About the world being your mirror."

"You've heard that too?"

Nathan nodded.

"Huh."

"And then, whatever we see in the mirror," Nathan said, "instead of reacting to it and rejecting it, love it." He couldn't believe what he was saying. Were those words coming out of *his* mouth?

"I'm hardly going to love myself for leaving Prue to carry the whole family," his father retorted. "For ducking my responsibilities and making this mess," waving a hand.

"Maybe it's not as bad as it looks. Maybe there's something good in it."

"Being irresponsible and chickening out of life – running out on *you*," his father said harshly. "How can there be any good in that?"

"Maybe you're going to find a different way of working that you like better," Nathan suggested. "Maybe you're going to end up healthier than you ever were to begin with. Maybe," he said, in a moment of brilliance, "maybe this is happening to you because you're extra *special*, not extra stupid – maybe it's something that only the most special people are chosen for."

Matt was frowning again. He looked away from Nathan to the papers on his desk and shifted a few of them around. He looked at the piles on the floor and the filing cabinet.

"Maybe you're scrunching right down into the bottom of yourself to get ready for a big leap," Nathan said intently. *When I am weak, then I am strong...* The words flashed across his mind. He set the office chair spinning wildly. "Maybe it's time for you to write the story you *want* to live, Dad. Time for you to Create instead of Reacting."

Matt looked up at him.

"You, Mage," Nathan declared, stopping abruptly. He pointed at his father with narrowed eyes and a straight arm. "Power of the Light, Dad. Your chance to choose."

Chapter 11

GROWING THROUGH IT

Nathan was still sleeping heavily when Prue knocked on his door. She knocked a few more times and then opened the door and looked in.

"Nathe. School. You've slept in, buddy." Coming to the bed, she rocked him by the shoulder. "Wake up, Sleeping Beauty."

He opened a bleary eye and regarded her balefully.

"Huge salad on the bench for your lunch," she added, turning to leave. "And fruit. And nuts. The chips and bickies are dead and gone."

He'd heard the garbage truck through his sleep haze – the mechanical grind and thud as all their yummy junk food was tipped into its bowels, to be crushed and pulverised.

Prue was switching the blender off when he entered the kitchen. She poured three tall glasses of something bright green.

"What the – is that?"

"Language!" she warned. "Green smoothie. Bananas and kale."

"What th – what's kale?"

"A vegetable. Kind of a cross between silver beet and cabbage."

His face expressed his feelings.

"Don't look like that," she said, holding out a glass. "It's a big hit of nutrition. Plant food is a powerful detoxer, and the chlorophyll in it has a similar structure to haemoglobin."

"Hemo-what?" he said, taking a wary step backwards and shaking his head.

"'Globin. Blood. Green foods purify and build blood cells."

She took a tentative sip, and then another. "It's not bad. Try. Think of it as superfood."

He was about to say 'no thanks' when he remembered his thought of the previous night: if *he* couldn't make changes, how could he expect his dad to?

It was okay. Not what he would call delicious, but not terrible either. And pretty filling, which was good because the cereal was all gone, the milk was gone, the bread was gone, and in their place was a saucepan with porridge.

"Sugar?" he asked hopefully.

"Cinnamon," Prue said. She glanced at the clock. "Dad's sleeping in late, too. Did you guys have a midnight party or something?"

He looked up but it was a completely innocent comment; she was on her way out of the kitchen.

Breakfast eaten, lunch box in hand, Nathan was

drawn toward his father's study. Opening the door he found the desk cleared and a stack of cardboard boxes lined up against the wall. Labels had been scrawled on each box in black marker pen: 'Bills', 'Jobs to invoice', 'Ideas', 'To file'... He closed the door quietly and went to his parents' room. Prue was just leaving.

"You're going to miss the bus," she said, kissing the top of his head.

"I'm riding," he replied. "Is Dad awake?"

"Barely."

He looked in. His father was lying on his back, mouth slightly open, eyes closed.

"Dad?"

Matt grunted.

"Good work."

Another grunt.

"Have a good day."

No answer.

"*Create* a good day," Nathan amended, pointing a Mage hand at his father's prostrate body.

"Have you brushed your teeth?" Prue asked from behind him.

He rolled his eyes and she followed him to the bathroom, saying, "I'm reading a very strange Cherry-book at the moment."

Nathan dumped his lunchbox on the floor and squeezed toothpaste onto his brush then met her eyes in the mirror.

"The author reckons that every single thing that happens is a balance of good and bad. Listen to this," sitting on the edge of the bath and flipping to a page: "'*Wellness results from the whole-hearted embrace of every event that befalls you.*' What do you make of that, Nathe, '*every* event'?"

He was brushing and full of foam so he couldn't speak, but it reminded him of Rada.

"'Wellness results from the whole-hearted embrace of *every* event that befalls you,'" Prue repeated. "Every event..."

"You should read that to Dad," Nathan mumbled through the foam, and then spat hurriedly, because it was starting to spurt out of his mouth.

"I will," she said, and headed back to their bedroom, still reading.

Nathan's class was supposed to be doing Ancient History but there'd been news that morning about civil war in Africa escalating, and a random comment sidetracked the whole class for ages. Listening to the passionate conversation around him about evil and how to stop it, Nathan found himself wondering if everyone was somehow missing the point.

If illness wasn't a mistake but instead some sort of feedback system for guiding the person back to health, then maybe war was similar. Maybe it wasn't about crushing the enemy but learning from them. Maybe the people who thought they were innocent and right had some waking up to do of their own. What if it wasn't about right and wrong at all – what if *everyone* needed to look in the mirror and own up to things they were denying or rejecting...?

He thought about the Harry Potter books, and how

everyone's efforts were focused on defeating Voldemort. But in the very end Harry had to surrender, not fight. He had to *own* the bit of Voldemort in him. When he did, things worked out – for him. (Not for Voldemort, who wasn't up for owning anything he didn't like.)

So maybe, Nathan thought, frowning, the classroom discussion now far from his awareness, maybe when there was a war going on, whether out in the world or inside your body, it was just a sign that things were out of balance, and so the first step was to be grateful for the wake-up call. Not to call the cancer a 'stupid lump' and try to cut it out. Not to call people 'terrorists' or 'evil', but to recognise that those things were all feedback that the system was out of balance, and then take responsibility – to realise that *you* created it, just as his dad had when he saw that the cancer was the result of his own anger and shame (and bad diet, Cherry would say), and to take care of it.

"Hitler!" Brett called out, bumping Nathan as he gave the Nazi salute.

"Mussolini!" someone else said.

"Pohl Pot." The Asian girl in front of Nathan and Brett said.

"Stalin."

"Magabe."

The whole class was clearly agreeing that these were evil people, but what if dictators only turned up because the people had *already* given their power away, rather than the other way around? What if the tyrants terrorising Africa were a symptom rather than a cause, just like the cancer? Surely dictators couldn't rise to power in a country full of empowered citizens...?

Nathan could see that most people wouldn't want that kind of responsibility. They would rather believe that things happened to them, and they were innocent, whether it was sickness or conflict, even though the balancing side of the argument was that if you could create horrible stuff, you could equally create great stuff. But most people wouldn't want that; they'd stay Reactors. Becoming a Creator was hard work. First, the responsibility side of things, and then you had to decide how you wanted it to end; you had to be a conscious player, a Mage, rather than falling for how it looked and just going with the flow. And *then* you had to take action, to change your diet or your attitude or your behaviour, or whatever was out of balance. And you had to hang in there and keep doing it even when it didn't seem to be working and it was taking forever and you weren't even sure you believed things could or would change. Like Gandhi and Mandela and landing on the moon.

But when you did all that, when you did hold the vision, you activated the Power of the Light: you were living a powerful Truth that could literally dissolve enemies.

They are back in the mirrored room, only this time Nathan's dad is sitting cross-legged on the floor with them, and Nathan is standing up talking to everyone. Outside the sounds of war continue – explosions and crashes and a heavy grinding sound that makes the whole room shudder and shake.

Suddenly the door bursts open and a Reactor stands there. It's a monstrous looking thing at first glance, but as they gaze at it, they see the thinnish man within it. He is frowning and waving his hands at them furiously and shouting, shouting. Nathan turns back to the group.

*"True power results from the whole-hearted embrace of **every** event that befalls you," he explains. "Instead of resisting it and reacting to it and calling it terrible and fighting it, you invite it in. You have a good look at it and you see how it serves you. For instance," he faces his dad, "how is being sick serving you?"*

"Yoohoo!" a voice calls cheerily from the door. It's Rada! She walks straight through the thin-man-Reactor, beaming at them all. "You figured out the Problem of Measurement! Excellent. Now the real work begins. But first – green smoothies for everyone!"

Chapter 12

THE REWARD

Nathan hadn't plonked in front of the TV for ages, it seemed. Not since Dad had become sick and taken over the couch for his day bed, and not since their home had become a place to escape from. Things were very different these days. There was no lasagne to plonk with, the fridge was chock full of vegetables and fruit, and while he missed his old diet, sitting down to a dish of fresh, juicy fruit was not too bad at all.

Nathan put the fruit bowl on the coffee table and tossed himself onto the couch. Choosing a ripe nectarine, he took a big bite, flicked the TV on with the remote, and started searching for something good to watch. He was becoming mildly absorbed in a show about inventions that had gone wrong, when the doorbell rang, and a moment later the door opened and Cherry called, "Anyone home?"

"In here," he called back, and he heard her moving through the house, depositing keys and something in the kitchen, and then coming into the lounge.

"Phew, nice and cool in here," she said, dropping into

an armchair and sticking long bare legs out in front of her. "There's a really lovely breeze but it's so hot whenever it stops. These first hot days after winter are a real shock to the system."

"You look brown," he commented, turning the volume down a bit.

"Happens when you spend time outside. Can I have one of those?"

"Sure." He held out the bowl and Cherry took a peach.

"Mum and Dad not back yet?"

"Nope."

She nodded, biting and quickly sucking to draw in the juice. "Mmmyum."

They were both chewing and gazing at the screen when Prue's Mazda rolled into the driveway. Car doors closed. Muffled voices spoke tiredly. The key turned in the back door and the sounds immediately grew louder: rustling plastic bags, shoes on tiles, a chair scraping against the floor, the fridge being opened.

"Let's help them. Sounds like they've brought shopping," Cherry said. She paused by the door and looked at Nathan intently. "Come on."

"Why?"

"To help," she mouthed, making a 'you dummy – isn't it obvious?' face.

Nathan sighed, procrastinated for as long as he could, and then lifted himself off the couch.

His father was sitting at the kitchen table, his head against the wall, his eyes closed. Prue was unpacking shopping into the fridge – yet more fruit and greens, and

Cherry was taking a big container out of her bag and talking.

"So I reckon he could be the one. He's been cancer-free for eight years now following this plan, and he's not that far away from you guys."

"Thanks, Cherry," Prue said from inside the fridge. "We'll look him up."

"Anything I can do?" Nathan asked from the doorway.

"No thanks, mate," his mother said. "Thanks for asking."

"Yes, there is," Cherry interjected. "Grab some plates and forks for everyone. I've brought the most amazing raw vegetable lasagne."

Matt's eyes opened. He looked at his sister wryly. "*Raw* lasagne?"

"Like, raw meat?" Nathan asked in horror.

"No, drongo. Raw vegetables and avocado and pesto sauce – things like that."

"Oh," Matt closed his eyes again. "Wake me when this nightmare is over."

Cherry shook her head.

"Sounds delicious," Prue said. "Thanks, Cherry."

"So, can I ask?" Cherry said, drawing out a chair. "How did it go?"

Prue glanced at her husband. "Pretty good really. There's no further growth. It hasn't shrunk but it's no bigger. They think that's a good sign. They said to keep doing what we're doing."

"That's great news!" Cherry enthused, and Nathan felt a leap in his chest and a smile blossoming on his face. "So why are you so flat today?"

"Just tired," Matt said, head still resting against the wall, eyes opening a little.

"It's all the toxins coming out of you," Cherry pronounced.

"He's trying not to get excited," Prue said in the same moment. "Just in case."

Nathan lifted a long, pointed arm toward his father and gazed at him through narrowed eyes. Matt looked back at Nathan through his own half-open eyes.

"Are you zapping him with good health?" Cherry asked, interested.

"It's something the two of them have been doing lately," Prue said, cutting herself a sloppy slice of raw lasagne. She dug her fork into the mixture and took a mouthful.

Nathan was sending his father a mental message: *Use the Power of the Light. Use the Power of the Light.*

Matt was sending one back: *Yeah, all right, mate. Give me a moment...*

"Hey, this is yum!" Prue enthused. "What's in it, Cherry?"

"Pesto, avocado, ultra thin slices of raw zucchini and spinach and a phenomenal raw tomato sauce... I'll send you the recipe." She hitched herself up onto a kitchen stool. "The thing I like best about eating this way is how you feel after: light and clean and balanced. You remember how I was wearing that spare tyre for years – since I was seventeen or so? You remember, Matt? Well, look," she put one hand on her hip and turned in a circle like a model. "All gone! Trim and slim."

He nodded, impressed. Even Nathan could see the difference.

Nathan was dismounting to follow the 'no riding in the school grounds' rule when Brett skidded to a stop beside him, almost crashing into the gravel at Nathan's feet, words burbling out of him as he leapt up and righted his bike.

"You know that hot chick – the new one?"

"Red hair?" Nathan asked.

"Yeah. She's –" he jerked his head behind him and Nathan turned. The new girl was walking her bike in through the gates and watching them. As soon as they looked in her direction, she glanced away.

"What about her?" Nathan asked.

"She likes you," Brett said, raising his eyebrows suggestively.

Nathan's gaze jerked back in the direction of the girl. She was looking at them again. She looked away at once.

"How do you know? Are you sure?

"Yep. Heard her telling Sal."

"Saying what?" Nathan asked disbelievingly.

"'Who's that cute guy who doesn't talk much?'" Brett said in his girly voice.

Nathan frowned and made himself not look back at her even though he was busting for a good, long stare. 'Doesn't talk much'. Was that good or bad?

The new girl, Gina, was hanging around near the teacher's desk when Nathan and Brett entered the classroom. Miss Walpole beckoned Nathan, waving a stapled assignment at him. "Lovely fantasy story, Nathan," she beamed. "I think you'll be very happy with your mark."

He took the pages, flushing, not sure where to look: at Miss Walpole who was smiling at him, or at Gina who was watching with interest, or should he grab the leering Brett by the shirt and drive him away from there?

"Can I read it?" Gina asked, and Nathan was so surprised that he stopped in his tracks.

"As for you, Brett," Miss Walpole murmured, looking through the stack of papers on her desk. "It started out very well, most promising, but then you just seemed to run out of steam..."

"Do you really want to?" Nathan asked Gina disbelievingly.

"Sure. I like fantasy stories."

"It's not really a fantasy," Nathan began to say, and then stumbled, "well, it sort of is, but..."

She held out her hand for the story, smiling. She had beautiful eyes – very blue. Her earrings were dangling golden angels with a tiny blue stone in them that perfectly matched her eye colour. You found yourself looking from the blue in her eyes to the blue in the stone and back again.

"I won't take long," Gina said. "I'm a quick reader."

"Okay." He dragged his gaze away from her eyes and her earrings, hesitated for another moment, and then smiled awkwardly and went to his seat. Brett was making goo-goo eyes at him and clutching his failed essay to his heart. Nathan gave him a sharp push and he thudded backwards into someone else, who fell against a desk and complained loudly.

Nathan is showing Gina around. She is very curious to see a Reactor but there isn't one anywhere near, it seems. "But if you start reacting to things, sooner or later you turn into a Reactor," he explains to her, as they cycle through the quiet countryside.

*"I really liked your fantasy story!" she calls to him, and then suddenly directs her bike right across his path, making him wobble dangerously. She shoots away off the path and down the hill. Nathan laughs, righting his bike, and beginning to chase her, when suddenly Brett is there in the chase too, and it all gets more serious. Nathan does **not** want Brett to win. He cycles harder, pushing his feet around and around until his muscles burn. Gina is still off ahead, her red hair flying behind her. Nathan pumps his legs harder and the next minute they are all flying off the grassy ledge into a vast lake, bikes and all. They splash and flail around and laugh and splutter, before swimming to the edge and dragging themselves out, dripping and weak with laughter. Rada is standing on the bank surrounded by the small group of Creators.*

"All right, it's time," she is saying. "You've seen what happens when people get caught in reaction. You've seen how the Reactors' numbers grow. Now it's time to forget about those Reactors and all of that shemozzle." She beams at them. "It's time to get really focused on what you want to Create and to build your beautiful dream some real foundations."

Nathan looks around the group. He sees the girl in overalls and the dark woman and the greyish-

haired man amongst them. The large woman calls out, "Build them how?"

"What, why, then how," Rada says. The phrase echoes in Nathan's mind: **what, why, then how**… He likes the sound of it. What, why, then how; what, why, then how; what, why, then how…

The sounds roll around and around in his mind, only fading when his eyes opened and that world melted away.

Chapter 13

THE ROAD BACK

Nathan braked outside their front driveway to check the letterbox: three envelopes and a plastic-covered magazine. He rode one-handed down the side of the house straight into his bike's under cover 'parking zone', climbed off, lifted his heavy schoolbag onto his shoulder, and backed into the house via the dodgy screen door. Prue was in the kitchen chopping vegetables. She was always chopping vegetables these days. Saying 'hi', he dropped the mail onto the table and was heading for his room when her response caught him by surprise. The knife clattered onto the wooden board and Prue darted straight to the table, grabbing the magazine and ripping its plastic cover off. She began to leaf through its pages feverishly, then, not finding what she was looking for, went back to the index page and ran her finger down the list.

"What are you looking for?" he asked, hovering in the doorway.

"Dad's..." she murmured; "Ah!" She turned a bunch of pages at once, then two more, and beamed.

Nathan shrugged and was about to move on when she declared triumphantly, "Look!"

Turning back, he saw that she was showing him an article and her finger was pointing to...? He squinted and came closer... his father's name. " 'By Matthew Cole,'" he read aloud and looked at her, puzzled. "So?"

She grinned and beckoned him to follow her, so he did, and they went outside to where his father was sitting in a patch of sun in the back yard. Nathan hadn't even seen him when he'd arrived home.

Matt was on the sun lounge, legs stretched in front of him, head turned to one side, eyes closed. He was breathing quietly, as if he was deeply asleep. He looked very peaceful, Nathan thought.

Prue bent over her husband, bringing her face close to his ear, and whispered something; his eyes opened immediately. He looked at her steadily, inscrutably. She held out the page to him and he took the magazine with a slight frown, read the first paragraph or two, looked at her again with a quizzical expression, and flipped it closed to see the front cover.

"Meet your new agent," she smiled, holding out her right hand.

"When – *how* did you do this?" he asked, sitting up but not taking her hand.

"Few weeks ago." Her arm dropped to her side. "I've submitted quite a few things of yours. That was a good tidy-up you did the other night. Made my job much easier."

"Your job? Prue –"

"Well, I don't have that much to do at the moment so

I thought I'd see if I could get your work out there. After all, I *am* a Marketing Manager." She was grinning, very happy with herself. "I was going to show you your new social media pages tonight."

"But how?" he asked, looking back at the magazine.

"LinkedIn. I've been networking in your industry, babe."

"Seriously?" His gaze went from the magazine in his hands to his wife and then to Nathan. There was an expression on his face that was hard to read. As if pleasure and displeasure were fighting for control.

"What's the matter?" she said flatly, hands on her hips. "You'd rather I not do this?"

"No!" he exclaimed. "Well..."

"What is it?"

"You're always..." another glance at Nathan... "rescuing me."

"It's called teamwork," she said tartly, turning on her heel. "But what would you know about that!" And she stalked off into the house, slamming the door behind her.

The air in the back yard buzzed. Matt heaved himself out of the sun lounge and followed her, giving Nathan's shoulder a slight squeeze as he passed. Nathan waited, expecting raised voices, but it was quiet in the kitchen. He moved slowly towards the back door, still hearing nothing, then opened it slowly, which always made it creak more.

His parents were standing in the middle of the kitchen, hugging. Matt had his arms tightly around Prue, and his face was buried in her hair. Prue's eyes were closed and Nathan saw wet streaks on her face. He walked past them quietly.

Over dinner, a huge salad full of ingredients that Nathan would never, *ever* have eaten willingly if it were not for his determination to support his dad, another conversation came up. It turned out that his parents had been to see the fellow Cherry had told them about the other day, a man who had been diagnosed with a really aggressive cancer and then healed himself, and who was now helping others. This crazy raw diet had been a big factor in his recovery too.

"It's so good to meet people who are positive!" Prue declared. She poured a sauce that she had just blended over the salad and licked her fingers. "Yum. I mean, people try to be positive everywhere but there's always this dead-end kind of feeling hanging around, whereas this guy is really certain, really certain that it's not a death sentence, and you run into clients in his waiting room who are actually recovering. I mean, it's not just a myth, it's not hokey, it's real."

"That's great!" Nathan enthused. He took a cautious mouthful of his salad. (Raw cabbage, raw corn, sprouts, apple, sunflower seeds, walnuts... weird!)

There was a knock at the kitchen door and Grandma poked her head in. "Don't get up," she said, opening the door wider and coming in. "I thought you'd be eating but I was just going past."

Grandma and Grandad didn't live anywhere nearby so this was a strange comment.

"Sit down," Prue said, pulling out a chair. "Would you like some salad?"

Grandma looked at the bowl doubtfully. "Oh no, that's all right, Prue. I've got dinner in the oven at home. I can't stay long."

She looked at Nathan brightly and patted his hand. "How are you, Nathe?"

"Okay," he replied through the mouthful (which tasted passable, actually).

"Good," she said, and then turned to Matt almost as if she hadn't heard him. "And you?"

Nathan's father gave a little nod. "Not bad."

"Good. Good," she said again. "And you, Pruey?"

"Great, thanks, Mum."

"Prue got me into one of the country's most prestigious publications." Matt lifted the magazine off the table and passed it to his mother. "Page 27."

"Well done," Grandma said, flicking through to the article. She began to read it, a little frown of concentration scuttling to and fro across her forehead.

The others chewed, watching her. This salad took a lot of chewing.

"May I take this home to read?" Grandma asked, looking up suddenly. "I have something on my mind and I can't seem to focus on your article right now."

"Sure," Matt said. "I'll make you a copy." He looked at his mother more closely. "What's up, Mum?"

"I just wondered if I could have a word," she said. "I don't mean to interrupt your dinner..."

"Go on," Prue said. "You two go into the dining room and have a chat."

"It's just that your father is struggling," Grandma said

gratefully. She stood up. "Bring your food."

"It can wait. It's not as if it's going to get cold." Matt followed her out of the kitchen. Alone, Prue and Nathan went back to chewing. Chewing and wondering what was being said next door.

"Well, at least they're not shouting," Prue said eventually. She pointed to the salad. "What do you think?"

"It's okay," Nathan replied. "My mouth still wants chicken and baked potatoes though."

She made a face. "Don't remind me... But actually, honestly, it's quite tasty, don't you think?"

"It's okay," he said again, evenly, and she grinned.

"Well, maybe you'll like the chocolate raspberry chia pudding I've made for dessert better."

"Sounds better," he said. "Chia?"

"These little seeds. They're superfood."

"Superfood!" Nathan shook his head in amazement. "I'm not six anymore, Mum."

Prue laughed. "I'm serious. That's what they're called."

Next door his father said loudly, defensively, "All right, I will!" and they heard Grandma saying, "Thank you, Matthew. That means a lot to me." And then Grandma was smiling brightly at them and kissing each cheek and waving from the door before hurrying home to rescue her dinner from the oven.

Matt stood by the sink, gazing out through the window after his mother. Sighing heavily, he came back to the table. Prue looked at him questioningly.

"Dad's depressed," Matt said abruptly. "Because of that conversation in the hospital ages ago. She reckons he's aged a lot – starting to lose track of what he's saying and doing. Looks like that's my fault."

"Would you stop the constant blaming and guilt trips!" Prue exclaimed. "Honestly!" She dropped her cutlery onto her plate and pushed it away. "So what does she want you to do?"

"Go see him," Matt said. "See if I can patch it up with him."

"Good," Prue replied. She crossed her arms and stared at him.

It was quiet in the kitchen. Matt looked from her to his salad and across to Nathan. Nathan was remembering their conversation in his father's office in the middle of the night: *"So all my life I've been pissed off with Grandad for being out of control of his drinking. And now I'm waking up to how out of control I've been..."*

Prue bounced out of her seat, grabbed the book she had been reading off the bench, and rifled through its pages. *"'Wellness results from the whole-hearted embrace of every event that befalls you,'"* she read. Then looked up. *"Every event."*

"You're all ganging up on me," Matt said after a moment. But he was fighting a smile.

"What if it's true?" Prue asked intently. "What if the only reason we get sick is because we're judging and resisting something?" She skimmed through the pages some more, and read, *"'Anger or resentment toward another poisons the self.'* That makes total sense!" she exclaimed, closing the book. "If we're tense and angry with someone else it's *our* body that's feeling tense and angry. And you've been mad with your dad for years – ever since you were a kid. It's no wonder it all backed up."

Matt took a mouthful of his salad and chewed slowly. Nathan watched them both.

"Okay," his father said. "You want me to find a way to... what...? Be grateful that he was a shit of a dad?"

"It's worth a try," she said. "Maybe you grew in a way that you might not have if he'd been the perfect dad. Him being a shit of a dad made you stronger, that's for sure – you stood up to him. And you became independent – you left home sooner. And you chose to be a really caring and committed father. That's got to count for something."

"Do not be a Re-ac-tor," Nathan intoned suddenly. "Be a Cre-a-tor." He raised his arm slowly, pointing at his father. "You, Mage."

Prue looked at them both strangely. "What the –?"

"Language," Nathan warned, without breaking his position. Prue shook her head, smiling.

"Power of the Light, eh?" Matt said. "The hidden blessings when you look into it more deeply."

"Yes," Nathan replied in his robotic tone. "Enlightened response." Then he switched back to his normal voice. "You know those martial artists that can fight lots of people all at the same time and they always know who's about to attack them just before they attack?" He leapt out of his chair and demonstrated fighting off ten attackers at once, crazily leaping and twisting and whirling around the kitchen. Prue pushed his chair in rapidly so he wouldn't collide with it.

"Yeah," Matt grinned, watching him.

"Well, you wouldn't be able to do that if you were

all locked-up and tense about defending yourself," Nathan puffed. "It would only work if you were really relaxed, just flowing with all the attacks like they didn't even mean anything." He began to flow his arms around and kick his legs with precision, as if he were masterfully disposing of the ten attackers.

"So?"

"So maybe every crap thing that happens in life is like one of those attackers and we can get tied up in knots trying to conquer them all or... we can dance with them," and he went back into his masterful martial arts demo against the invisible attackers. "Not reacting or resisting or making them wrong..."

"You're onto something, buddy," Prue said admiringly.

"Got an example of your own?" Matt queried. "What's *your* personal challenge at the moment?"

Nathan stopped leaping and looked his father in the eye. "You."

Chapter 14

RADOS

It was as if his father had a full-time job to get well. Every day Matt was busy from the time he got up till the time he went to bed following this new regime the health food guy had given him. He was eating masses of raw fruit and drinking green smoothies and fresh juices and lying in the sun, going for walks, taking Epsom Salt baths, and – really gross – *enemas*, where you pumped water up your bum to clean yourself out! Ugh! Gross... And – not so bad – he was brushing his skin with a natural-bristle brush, having massages, watching comedies and funny movies, and sitting with his eyes closed, meditating and visualising himself being healed. And he'd started putting signs up around the house, like the Arnold Schwarzenegger quote now pasted to the bathroom mirror that read, '*Strength does not come from winning. Your struggles develop your strengths. When you go through hardship and decide not to surrender, that is strength.*'

Nathan enjoyed reading the quote aloud in Arnie's

tone of voice and accent. One day, while he was brushing his teeth, he realised that this quote and *'For when I am weak, then I am strong'* were essentially saying the same thing. It was as if there was a secret purpose in life's challenges to make people grow, so long as you didn't turn into a Reactor and freak out or run away...

Prue was doing most of the new regime with Matt, and when she wasn't, she was in his office busily spruiking his articles and stories to various publications. She even started wearing her tight suits and crazy-heel shoes again because they made her feel like she was properly at work. Matt was stunned by her success rate compared with his. "It's because this is my specialty," she would say, rolling her eyes at his stupidity, but they could both see how pleased she was. "You'll have to start writing again soon or I'll run out of material to sell," she added, and that got Nathan's father thinking about doing a series of articles on cancer and the various treatments that were available, and interviewing people who had overcome it.

Friends and neighbours had stopped dropping off casseroles, mainly because now most people knew they were eating raw and for some reason they figured that raw meals were easier to prepare so no extra help was needed, even though Prue was spending hours every day chopping and blending and juicing. But Nathan could now honestly tell the ones who asked that his dad was much better. The heavy feeling had lifted. Life was feeling normal again.

The only thing Matt hadn't done yet was speak to Grandad. He said he'd tried to make a time and Grandad had put him off.

"So you wimped out," Prue said bluntly, hands on her hips.

"I don't feel up to driving all the way over there," Matt said, "and he won't come here."

"Okay. Leave it with me," and Prue turned on her heel smartly and switched the blender on so that Matt's objection was drowned out.

In fact, Nathan had relaxed so deeply into the 'everything's all right now' place that when he arrived home from school one day to find his dad barfing into the toilet and his mum looking really stressed in the kitchen, the old fears and anxiety were back instantly, like a huge tsunami wave engulfing everything, roaring through their lives with the power to destroy everything within seconds.

"What's wrong with Dad?" he asked.

Prue looked up from the fruit she had been chopping, a frown still etched on her forehead. "He's having what they call a 'healing crisis'," she said, "when the toxins are being released out of the body and it makes you sick. He'll be all right." But she didn't look convinced, and later that night Nathan discovered that one of the women at the health centre they'd been attending, who was doing all the same things as his father, had just died. So if this wasn't going to work either, what would?

The old dark shadow had edged back into the house, following his father who was creeping like an old man between the bathroom and his bedroom, looking pale and sweaty, stopping to hang onto the wall at times and not even noticing Nathan, who stood in a doorway watching him. It didn't occur to Nathan to say, 'You, Mage', but even if he had, his father would probably have made a tired, 'not now' gesture, and toppled into bed, eyes closing immediately.

Nathan was torn between escaping to Brett's and staying to help his father, although what he could possibly do, he didn't know. Sitting on the floor in his room, his back against the wardrobe, he stared at the opposite wall with its posters of sport stars and science fiction movie characters, and wondered when this nightmare was going to end for good, when life would be truly normal and you wouldn't have to walk on eggshells in case the good times didn't last.

He hadn't sat on the floor in here for ages, he reflected, seeing his bed and desk and window from the new perspective. There was a piece of paper poking out from under his bed and he reached forward to see what it was. Another few sheets came with it; they were stapled together. It was his Rados story. Brushing cobwebs off it, he read the beginning and then got caught up in it and read the rest.

"It's because you understand the idea but you still want everything to be nice," Rada says gently. *She is holding his hands between hers and they are sitting close, looking into each other's eyes. There is no one else there, just the two of them in the field, sitting on the grass.*

"The Reactors take form when we resist what is, when we refuse to see the blessings in how things are,"

she continues. "But as soon as we see the blessings, they dissolve, just as you saw."

"So I'm still Reacting…" Nathan says, and Rada nods. "Then what does the Problem of Measurement have to do with it?" he asks, perplexed.

"How you measure it is how you see it," she explains. "See it as a disaster and you'll unleash **that** experience; see it as an opportunity or a gift, and you'll unleash that experience."

Nathan takes a deep breath, contemplating this. Right now, he feels safe and loved, as if nothing will ever go wrong again, as if he can relax and drift in this warm, comfortable place forever, just the two of them, smiling at each other… But some part of him knows that thought is 'off'. He is here **to be** challenged. He is here to turn the Power of the Light onto whatever happens: to not resist; to not fight; to love and appreciate, and to Create what he wants to experience.

He looks down at their interlocked hands and notices that his forearms are much stronger and more muscular than usual. So are the thighs and calves of his crossed legs. Even his voice has changed, he realises; it's deeper.

"If we wait for anything outside of ourselves to make us happy, we are not following the Quantum Law," Rada says. "We are relying on the outer to change the inner. We have to become happy and grateful **first**. Trying to manifest what you want is ineffective because the state of wanting is a state of lack; you can only bring into being what you already have. Creators *create their desired state within themselves first."*

Nathan nods. It's quite clear now.

"I've taken a good honest look at my life," he hears himself saying, only it is not his voice, but his father's, that is speaking. "I've seen how I was giving up and running out on myself and my family. I've decided to stay and grow through it."

"What did you say?" his mother asked fiercely.

"I said, all right! I'll stay and go through it!" Matt replied in a low, harsh voice.

Nathan opened his eyes. He was slumped against the wall of his bedroom, head hanging down over one shoulder, drool wetting his chin and cheek. Grimacing, he wiped the drool away with the back of his hand, then lifted his head too quickly and winced as pain shot through his stiff neck.

Outside in the hallway, his parents were still arguing.

"I forgot, okay?" Prue was hissing. "I invited them last week when you were well. I completely forgot they were coming today!"

"Well, it's too late to do anything about it now," Matt grumbled. "But I can already see how this is going to go. I'll be throwing up between each sentence and Dad's going to get on his friggin' high horse and tear shreds off me again for being weak and useless!"

"Would you just listen to yourself!" Prue exclaimed, and then the doorbell rang. "Go and get dressed," she said quietly. "I'll bring them in and make tea."

Matt didn't say anything. Nathan could hear him shuffling away while Prue walked toward the front door and opened it with a falsely cheerful, "Hi! Lovely to see you – it's been ages."

Moving his neck around gingerly, Nathan raised his shoulders and stretched to ease out the cricks, then stood up and went to the door. He opened it quietly and walked to his father's room, hearing voices at the other end of the house. Matt was sitting in his pyjama pants on the edge of the bed, slowly buttoning a fresh shirt. He looked terrible.

"Grandma and Grandad?" Nathan asked.

Matt looked up. He nodded.

"Your big moment," Nathan said with a grin, punching the air like a hero. "Time to own the mirror and love him for being a shit dad."

For a moment Matthew said nothing, then a tear oozed out of his eye. He held an arm out to Nathan, who went and sat next to him, and they hugged.

"Thanks, mate," his father murmured. "Thanks."

Chapter 15
THANK YOU FOR-GIVING

Grandad was sitting in an armchair gazing at the floor when Nathan entered the lounge room. He didn't even glance up.

Grandma said brightly, "Look! It's Nathan!" and she gave Grandad's arm a little prod. Grandad's eyes trailed a zigzag route up from the floor until his gaze met Nathan's. He looked old and tired, as if the fight had gone out of him.

"Hey, Grandad," Nathan said, coming closer to kiss his cheek. "It's good to see you."

"Yes, isn't it?" Prue exclaimed. "We got so caught up here... we really lost track of how long..."

Matthew appeared in the doorway and everyone turned to observe his reaction when he saw his father. There was the flicker of something in his eyes, but it was unclear what.

"Hello, Mum," he said, advancing into the room and kissing her, then reaching a hand out to his father. "Dad."

Grandad looked at him, not lifting an arm to shake. Matt hesitated for a moment, and then reached further, wrapping his arm around his father's back and resting his face next to his for a moment, as if in a kiss.

The room breathed again.

Matt sat down. "What tea is this? It smells good."

"Lemongrass, ginger and mint," Prue said, pouring him a cup. "There's ordinary too."

"Dad and I have ordinary," Grandma said. "I guess that means *we're* just ordinary!" she added with a laugh.

"Not at all!" Prue babbled. "We're just being a tad extraordinary at the moment." She stopped, embarrassed.

"I never copied that article for you, Mum," Matt said into the pause.

"I'll do it!" Prue jumped up. "Nathe, come and give me a hand."

Nathan looked at her strangely but she stared back at him so intently that he followed without saying a word. In his father's office he closed the door behind them and said, "You don't need a hand."

"And we don't need to be in there right now. We'll give them a moment." She switched the computer and printer on and sat in Matt's office chair while they warmed up. Nathan perched on the spare swivel.

His mother had clearly been at work in here. There was a big calendar fixed to the wall with coloured post-it notes stuck to it, and a cheerful fringe of post-it notes tacked along the top of the computer.

"Can you really make enough money sending out Dad's articles?" he asked.

"I'm not sure. I'm still sussing it out," she replied, leaning forward to click her way through his computer files to the relevant article. "But I've started looking for work again for me, too – something part-time for now. Oh! Silly me. She'll want a copy of the real thing." Rolling in her chair to the big metal filing cabinet, Prue yanked out a drawer and pulled hanging files forward until she found the one that held the magazine she was seeking. She flicked through it for Matt's article then laid it in the scanner. The machine droned as it selected the area of the page for scanning.

"Grandad looks awful, doesn't he?" Nathan said.

Prue frowned and nodded. "No wonder Grandma's worried."

"But it's not Dad's fault," Nathan pressed. "Grandad made himself get depressed, didn't he?"

"Of course," his mother agreed. She lifted the lid of the scanner and turned the article for the second page. "It was, but relationships are everything, Nathe. There's no life without them. And if you can't create good ones with the people closest to you, well..." She clicked 'scan' again and swivelled to face him. "Did you know that when people are facing death the thing that almost everyone wants to do is to get in touch with the people they care about and say, 'I love you'? They don't want to finish their latest project or anything else. They just want to say, 'I love you and it's okay. Whatever happened, it's okay.'"

Nathan pushed his feet against the ground and spun around. Once. Twice. Three times. The office swam past – bookshelves, boxes, filing cabinet, desk, Mum, bookshelves, boxes, filing cabinet... He imagined what it would look like if he went *really* fast, if it all blurred together in one long mish-mash of colour. If you went fast, things that looked separate lost their edges and started to join up, like those black-and-white picture books that became grey when you turned the pages rapidly. If you went super-warp fast, maybe you would be everywhere at once; maybe time and space would disappear... Maybe you could move so fast that you'd *stop* moving, or be still-and-moving at the same time, like the centre of a roundabout...

"Nathan, stop it! You're going to wreck that chair!"

Using his feet as brakes, Nathan slowed down in jerks.

"Come on." Prue switched everything off and stapled the copied article. "Let's see if World War III has broken out in the lounge room..."

On their way back the doorbell rang again and they could see Cherry's head through the little side window. Prue let her in and the two women had an eye-to-eye conversation while their voices greeted each other.

In the lounge room, Matt and his parents were sitting in silence. Cherry breezed in and kissed everyone and commented on the weather and the crazy driver she'd been stuck behind and the fabulous pair of boots she had just found in an op shop. Under cover of her chatter, Prue turned to Grandma with a questioning expression. Grandma shrugged and gave a very slight shake of her head. Prue frowned. She leaned toward her husband and hissed, "Well?"

Matt looked at her irritably and gave a very slight shake of his head. "Let me do this my way," he muttered.

"This year or next?" she retorted under her breath, and he glared at her.

Picking up on the undertone, Cherry's voice trailed

away, and into the quiet Grandad asked, "Is it time to go?"

Prue said immediately, "Oh, don't go yet! I've got snacks!" She disappeared into the kitchen with Cherry on her heels.

Grandma said resignedly, "I'll give them a hand," and she left too.

Nathan hesitated. His father was staring at Grandad, who had returned to his position, gazing at the floor. They both looked at him. He was just an old man now, not the bully Matt remembered from his childhood. All of his strength and bluster seemed to have trickled out of him.

"Dad," Matt said suddenly.

Grandad was jerked out of his daydream. He looked up anxiously.

"What I said in the hospital that day," Matt continued, his expression and tone intent, "it was unfair. I've been as weak as you, in my own way. You saw my weakness and I saw yours. We're square."

Nathan was watching his grandfather. He didn't seem to be registering what his son was saying.

"In fact," Matt added heavily, "if it wasn't for you being exactly the way you were, I wouldn't be the man I am today. With the wife I have and the son I have." He glanced at Nathan with a smile that suddenly brimmed with tears, and then lifted himself out of his seat and went to sit next to his father, where Grandma had been sitting. Putting a hand on Grandad's forearm, he said, "You gave me some crap and some good stuff, and out of all of that I made a life. You might not like what I made, just as I didn't like what you made, and God knows I've made a mess, but I'll get it together."

"We all make a mess," Grandad said in a dry, raspy voice. He laid his old wrinkled hand on top of Matt's, and that was how they were sitting when Prue, Grandma and Cherry came in with the fruit platter.

The mirrored room is full to bursting. It's as if the word has got out that there's a way of not being controlled by Reactors, or maybe people are finally seeing through them. There's a real buzz in the room as Nathan walks around, looking for a face he knows.

The girl in overalls grabs his sleeve. "Hey! I created myself being friends with my sister again and it worked! Look – she's over there!"

He beams, and follows her pointing finger to where a girl with similar features is chatting in a small group.

*"How did **you** go?" Overalls-Girl asks him.*

"Dad's getting better," he says. "It's up and down but he's been looking in the mirror and starting to love. I think I helped."

She beams right back at him and raises a hand in a high-five. He meets her hand with a loud clap and they both grin.

Rada's voice catches their attention as she calls her usual, "Yoohoo! Everyone!"

The group gradually stops talking and turns to face her. She is standing on a chair so that she can be seen, and smiling so warmly at everyone that she seems to be putting out a light of her own.

"**What?**" she calls out loudly, and the crowd bursts into speech, all answering her at the same time but all saying different things.

Nathan looks at the girl next to him in confusion.

"What are you Creating?" she yells over the hubbub. "You know – what we were just talking about!"

"Oh," he says, still not quite sure.

Then, "**Why?**" Rada shouts, and as one, the group choruses back, "To own the mirror and be Creators rather than Reactors! To love ourselves and everyone and everything that happens! To dissolve Reactors and transform!"

Rada beams. "But **how?**" she asks, as if she has no idea, and they call out as one, "By the Power of the Light!"

The whole group erupts into cheering and clapping and laughter, and then Rada waves her hands for attention again. "But..." she says seriously, "what about the Reactors? Are we going to wipe them out?"

"No!" everyone yells.

"Why not?" she asks, pretending dismay.

"Because we'll always React," someone calls out.

"Then what's the point?"

"To bring light to it faster and faster!" someone else yells.

"To take what we are given and Create what we want!" a familiar voice says, and Nathan turns around in time to see the beautiful dark woman before she melts back into the crowd.

"What we're **given**?" Rada asks intently.

The woman reappears and waves a hand in acknowledgement. "You are correct: not 'given'; what we had previously Created."

"Ah…" Rada says, and she smiles. Then a quizzical expression crosses her face. "But… **how?** Doesn't your Creation need a plan?"

"Yes!" they call, and immediately everyone gathers into small groups, sitting on the floor and talking earnestly.

"What's happening now?" Nathan asks Overalls-Girl.

"If you don't have a plan, you're vulnerable to Reactors," she explains, beckoning him to join her group. "You've got to come up with a strategy, an action plan, or your dream is just a complete fantasy. For instance, me: I visualised getting on with my sister and I thought through what I wanted to say to her that wouldn't make either of us wrong. No Reacting! Then I went to see her."

Nathan squeezes into the huddle. Several people share a dream of building a school that will teach the children of this place how to Dream and Create. They are brainstorming ideas – how they will speak to the parents and inspire them and demonstrate how to Create and show them how to dissolve Reactors… A young man has the dream of interplanetary travel. He will have to study and become fit and sign up for courses that will qualify him to eventually join a space program... *A dark-skinned woman declares her intention to inspire the world to look beyond skin colour and racial and religious differences to the things people have in common. Instead of reacting to appearances, she wants people to be conscious of their essential connection as humans... Another woman tells them excitedly that everyone and everything is light! That we communicate by light – conversations are put into waves and particles and travel between us at the speed of light. She wants to learn everything about light and then she will teach others so they don't fall prey to Reactors. Power of the Light!*

*They ask Nathan what his Dream is, what **he** wants to Create. He looks around the circle of faces, wondering. On the far side of the room, Rada catches his eye and smiles. He smiles back, and instantly, he knows.*

Chapter 16

A NEW DREAM

Brett and Nathan were all set for an afternoon of gaming. Nathan was not only very happy with his new warrior character, named Rados, but he was also holding back a bubbling tide of excitement. Gina was going to join them. They had introduced her to the game and she had created a character – a sexy woman with blazing eyes and feather-woven, long, thick, black hair. Her character wore tight-fitting leather and high boots and armbands with jewels studded in them, and her name was Tareetha. He was so glad he had done away with the troll...

Brett had brought his laptop and when Gina arrived the three of them were going on a quest together. But at the back of Nathan's mind was another quest. He'd woken up the other day with the idea to develop a game of his own. It would be based on his Rados story and the dreams he'd been having about a world where 'Reactors' were taking over and the people were hiding to avoid them while they built up their strength as 'Creators'. Nathan didn't know the first thing about how to create a game but he was fired up by this idea and keen to learn. Brett's older brother was a bit of an expert – he'd created a game of his own that already had the beginnings of an online following, and he'd said he would show Nathan what to do.

The doorbell rang and Nathan leapt to answer it. Prue was blending in the kitchen so she hadn't heard, and Matt was out for a walk. "Here comes the girlfriend!" Brett chortled from the lounge room.

"Shut up!" Nathan hissed. He opened the door. Gina was standing on the step, smiling shyly.

"Come in – we're in here." He stood back and she entered, clutching her laptop bag and looking around. It was the first time he'd had a girl over and it felt strange. Nice-strange.

Gina set up her laptop and he showed her where the power outlet was, and the three of them began to talk about the quest they'd chosen. They each had different powers and different goals. Brett was always focused on building his store of treasure while Nathan was intent on building Rados's skills and abilities and Gina was just getting her character established. This quest was going to take them into new territory as they gathered a number of critical items, fought off enemies, and conquered difficult terrain.

It was the usual thing, Nathan mused; the conquering, the battles, the division into good and evil. He wondered what it would take to devise a game that would show people how to dissolve conflict by welcoming it rather than resisting it... For a moment, his imagination ran away with him, and he had a vision of his game taking off around the world, showing people how to be Creators, and even influencing how the real world worked so that actual conflict lessened and people who were sick were able to transform their health, like his dad was doing...

Prue's phone rang and he heard her answering it in the kitchen, and then the back door opened as Matt returned from his walk and their two voices mumbled and murmured and intertwined.

"That's pretty good news about your dad," Brett said.

Gina looked up.

"His dad was really sick," Brett explained. "Cancer, right?"

Nathan nodded. "Yep."

"Did he have to have operations and chemo?" Gina asked sympathetically.

"Yeah. Ages ago," Nathan said, "but since then he's been doing natural stuff and he's getting better."

"Cool," she said. "My uncle died of cancer a few years ago. It was really sad. I still miss him."

"It's an epidemic," Brett said. "There are masses of people with cancer these days. Weird."

"Junk food, chemicals, pollution, stress, EMFs," Nathan counted them off. "It's crazy to expect to be healthy and have all that stuff going on."

"Yeah but we can't stop it," Brett said matter-of-factly. "That's just life now."

"You don't have to eat crap. You can eat healthy."

Brett made a face. "Yeah but it tastes like crap."

"Not all of it," Nathan contradicted.

"Hey!" Gina exclaimed. "I've just realised that your

character is called Rados – like the one in your story."

"What story?" Brett asked.

"You know, the one Miss Walpole liked?"

Brett shrugged, not remembering.

"It's about this world where Reactors are taking over," Gina remembered. "It was good. I liked it. And Rados was the leader."

"Yeah." Nathan hesitated for a moment and then cast caution to the winds. "I'm thinking of creating a game about it. Brett's brother is going to help me."

"Cool," she said again. "Can Tareetha be in it?"

"Sure," he replied. Brett made goo-goo eyes and he flushed and ignored him. "It's going to be the sort of game where people don't just kill and conquer each other. Instead of reacting to dangers and problems they win points when they see them as allies and gifts."

"What's the point of that?" Brett demanded. "Takes all the fun out of it."

"Dying isn't fun," Gina objected.

"It's still going to be challenging," Nathan said. "They'll be faced with all the usual evil characters and tyrants and bad magic but instead of winning by killing, you win by transforming. There'll be a mirror that makes you face the dark forces in yourself, and then you go on a quest to become a Mage and learn how to transform the challenge."

"Whatever," Brett shrugged. "Can we get started on this game or what?"

Embarrassment flushed Nathan's cheeks and anger tightened his stomach. His delicate new idea had been brushed aside as if it was worthless. "Sure," he said woodenly, resolving not to talk about it again.

They were well into their game when he realised that he was still feeling hurt and humiliated, which meant that *he* had turned into a Reactor. *You've got to be able to do this yourself,* he told himself.

In his mind, he imagined a big, gold-framed mirror standing in front of him, and as he stared at his reflection he saw himself being as dismissive as Brett had just been. He'd been dismissive when his father first got sick, pushing him away because he didn't want to know, didn't want to feel the pain; he just wanted to get on with his own life and feel normal. It was as if a tendril of guilt had bound him to that quality, bringing it back to him for healing.

So, if he were to play his game right now... he would have to own that part of him and see how it served...How *did* it serve? He frowned in thought and then realised that his dismissiveness had protected him from pain until he was ready to face it and deal with it. Nathan sensed a lifting, a lightening of his mood as this thought settled into his mind. In that case, how had Brett's dismissiveness served *him*? And again, the answer came: it protected Brett from ideas he wasn't ready for either. And perhaps from jealousy that Nathan had come up with an original game idea and he hadn't, and that his brother had been so interested in it...

Nathan was no longer a Reactor but he had yet to become a Creator, a Mage. What would make him into a Creator?

"Oy!" Brett said, elbowing him. "Earth to Nathan. Are you playing or what?"

"Yeah." He focused on the game and made his move, all the while still thinking about what he could do in this real-life game to respond as a Creator, as a Mage. Was it as simple as just choosing to respond instead of react? Was it as simple as saying, 'Thank you for challenging me because that makes me grow?' Could it be that simple?

Immediately, he knew that it was. A thought like that brought light, *enlightenment*, into the dynamic, and immediately it began to transform. He sat up straighter, stronger, more resilient, ready for the next challenge.

"She seems like a lovely girl," Prue remarked, after Gina and Brett had left.

"Yeah," he agreed non-committally. "Is there any food? I'm starving!"

"I've saved you a slice of the raw cheesecake," she said. "It's on the bench."

"Thanks!" These raw food cheesecakes had no cheese in them at all, or sugar, but they were delicious. "Dad," Nathan said, taking the plate. "I've got an idea for a game. Can you help me?"

"Sure," Matt said. "What kind of game?"

"Based on that story I wrote."

"Tell me more."

"Before you start on that," Prue interrupted, "there are two things I've been meaning to tell you. Do you remember that girl being treated by Malcolm, the girl doing the whole fasting-raw-food-thing who died? Well, I was just talking to someone who went to her funeral. It turns out that she had a huge, unresolved feud going on with her mother for years – she was bitter towards her mum right up to the day she died."

"So?" Matt said.

"Well, it makes sense: doesn't matter how much raw food and goodness you load in if you're feeling angry and bitter all the time, because those kinds of feelings make your cells go primitive."

"'Go primitive'? Seriously, Prue."

"I *am* being serious! I was reading about it this morning. Big charged emotions make your cells go backwards to a more primitive state. It's called 'devolution' – opposite of evolution," she told Nathan.

"Duh," he said.

She made a face at him. "I didn't get it at first, Mr Brain. It's not that we shouldn't ever be angry, of course. Anger can be really useful for getting yourself moving; the problem is if you get stuck in it. So according to this book, love creates evolution, where your cells become more organised and efficient, and big charged emotions make your cells more primitive, which often means illness, and ultimately death if you never clear the emotion." She tapped Matt on the nose. "Lucky you patched it up with your dad."

"Yeah, but I'm still pretty mad with you," he said darkly, then caught her arm and drew her close. "Or maybe it would be more correct to say, 'mad about you.'"

Prue smiled, nestling against his chest.

"Seriously," Matt said, "I want to thank you for everything you've done to get me back on track. Both of you. If it wasn't for you two..." He shook his head grimly.

"Don't even go there," Prue said. "All that matters is that you're on the mend."

"You, Mage," Nathan intoned, with his pointed arm.

"You, bloody helpful," Matt retorted. "Come here." He pulled Nathan into their hug. "I love you guys."

"We love you," Prue sniffed, and Nathan felt a warm prickly buzz in his nose, as if he was about to cry too. It was worth it, he thought. The pain and fear and darkness. If you were willing to grow through it, it was worth it.

"Okay," Prue said, wiping her hand across her nose. "Don't make me messy. I'm going to an interview, remember?"

"Go on then," Matt said, whacking her on the backside as she moved away. "Good luck, babe."

She stuck a thumb in the air and headed out.

Keeping his arm around Nathan's shoulders, Matt led him into the lounge room. "Okay, mate, tell me all about this game idea of yours."

Health, Healing, 'Dis-ease', Regeneration, Power

The idea that the cause of disease is mysterious is the greatest myth of all time. Health and healing are very straightforward, but the vast machinery of government and corporate funding of medical research have over-complicated the simple essence of health and caused it to become tangled in vested interests.

There is not a multiplicity of diseases; there are certainly not 7000 'rare diseases'. 'Diseases' do not exist. They are labels assigned to a set of symptoms by the medical community in order to legally treat those symptoms with pharmaceutical drugs.

It is, however, impossible to *cure* when treating symptoms because the cause is not addressed. Despite all the money spent on medical research and all the new treatments and 'breakthroughs', cancer rates continue to skyrocket (from one in approximately 740 in 1908, according to the Australian Bureau of Statistics, to one in two in 2020), and each new virus or dis-ease 'requires' its own vaccine or pharmaceutical. Never mind that the 'cure' often causes the illness it claims to prevent (or others that are just as bad or worse), never mind that the side effects of the treatment are often worse than the disease itself...

It is well known by those schooled in the healing arts that most illness has a simple cause, and the means of healing is simply to eliminate the toxins that are responsible for all illness and replace them with clean wholefoods and natural products.

Unfortunately, the genuine caring and commitment of

many health professionals has been undermined by medical training that is funded by an industry focused on profit and removed from simple humane care. Scientific fervor results in many excessive and unnecessary medications and interventions. Each year more than 500 drugs are recalled because of the damage and death they cause. Whether it's medical errors, prescription errors or unnecessary surgeries, iatrogenic disease (illness caused by medical examination or treatment) is right up there with heart disease and cancer as a leading cause of death.

Instead of risking becoming caught in the endless complications generated by drugs, seek a health practitioner who works *with* the body and nature. When choosing this practitioner, consider the following criteria: rather than being guided by the person's title or qualifications or the prestige of their school, be guided by the person's *healing track record*, by the person's ability to:

- restore health and vitality,
- reverse disease (including 'terminal disease'),
- heal genetic and chronic conditions, and even
- regenerate organs that were surgically removed.

'A miracle healer?' you ask.

No, merely someone who understands how the body works, how nature works, and how to work with those principles.

In fact, anyone can understand and apply those principles, and in doing so can reverse their own disease and begin to restore health. In many cases a practitioner's support will be required because each succeeding generation is becoming weaker as a result of highly processed diets, artificial foods and drinks, pharmaceuticals, and exposure to toxic chemicals and EMFs in the environment and in many of our daily-use products and services. If the genetic 'slate' is not wiped clean through healing, cleansing and regenerative practices, this load is passed on to subsequent generations, which can make the healing process longer and more complex.

We are weakening our gene pool by not understanding these principles, and by choosing to prioritise temporary taste-pleasure or convenience over our long-term vitality, energy, health and capacity to regenerate.

Health – in a nutshell:

1.   All 'disease' or illness comes down to the health of the cell.

2.   Cellular health is determined by the terrain in the body.

3.   The terrain is determined by the quality of nutrition coming into the body and the efficiency of waste leaving the body. *(It's also determined by the quality of our thoughts. Our mind has the power to literally change our chemistry. The emerging field of epigenetics reveals that thoughts determine which genes are switched on and which remain dormant.)*

4.   Physical nutrition comes into the body via food and

beverage.

5.   Waste leaves the body via four channels of elimination: the kidneys/bladder (urine), the bowels (excrement), the skin (perspiration) and the lungs (respiration).

6.   There are two fluids in the body: blood, which carries nutrients to the cells, and lymph, which carries cellular waste to the four channels of elimination. The lymph nodes are 'septic tanks'.

7.   When waste is unable to be properly eliminated from the body, from either the intestines or the cells, it builds up and creates a toxic load and condition known as 'acidosis'.

8.   In a very minute percentage of the population, illness is caused by excess alkalinity, but in most cases it is caused by excess acidity.

9.   Certain foods and lifestyles create acidity and others create alkalinity.

10. Meat, dairy, grains, refined sugars and cooked foods create an acidic ash in the body. These foods are mostly 'dead' and therefore do not energise the body.

11. Fruit and raw vegetables are live foods that are alkalising. They have an electrical charge that energises the body.

12. Acidity causes pain, inflammation, swelling, hardness and dryness. Any of those symptoms indicates acidity.

13. The human race originated in tropical climates where nature provided an abundance of cooling (alkalising) fruit to balance the (acidic) heat. As humanity moved further afield into colder climates, we sought more warming (acidic) foods. Unfortunately, these foods create a toxic environment in the body and, consequently, disease.

14. The foods most healing to the body are fruits; next best is raw salads and vegetables. For maximum health and regeneration, the diet should be 80% raw fruits and vegetables. Ideally, the final 20% should be comprised of raw nuts and seeds (that have been soaked), and avocadoes. Grains and legumes are best avoided or eaten rarely, refined foods never. Meat and dairy are extremely acidifying and hard on the digestive system and kidneys.

15. Despite the widespread belief in the importance of (animal) protein, in reality many proteins are detected as foreign and are attacked by the immune system, causing inflammation (mucus). Protein does not generate muscle strength, as is commonly believed. The essential building blocks of protein, amino acids, are plentiful in fruits and vegetables. There are many Olympic-level plant-food-eating bodybuilders, weightlifters and athletes.

16. Humans were designed to be frugivores. Our physiology indicates this. We are more like chimps (frugivores) in appearance than dogs (omnivores), cows (herbivores) or tigers (carnivores). We don't have the instinctive desire to run down a deer, rip its flesh open with our sharp teeth, tear out its guts and eat

them raw and dripping with blood. We don't have the extra stomachs to digest the cellulose in many high-fibre greens, and therefore should prioritise easily digested fruits.

17. The sugar found in fruit, fructose, is a simple sugar that is easily digested and provides fuel for the body. Complex sugars, like sucrose, maltose and dextrose, are mucus forming and hard on the body's digestive system.

18. We were not designed to drink milk after being weaned, and certainly not the milk of another species. After age two, humans do not produce lactase, the enzyme required to digest milk, and so the body responds to it as a toxin. It forms mucus that clogs the lymphatic system and digestive tract.

19. Grains, legumes and beans are cheap and tasty but also have an acidic effect on the body and are difficult to digest.

20. Take even one step in the direction of greater health: eat fruit for breakfast!

21. Raw fruits and vegetables have an electrical charge; this charge is *light*; light is our truest and best form of nutrition. This is why people can go on extended fasts (eg. 40+ days) on water and/or fruit, and thrive.

22. But what about people on a bad diet who lived to a 'ripe old age' and were relatively healthy? We must never under-estimate the role of attitude and life purpose in our health. Loving, inspired, enthusiastic states of mind can transmute the effect of toxic foods. Another critical

factor is the physical environment – living in pristine areas can make a big difference, and, of course, there is our genetic inheritance.

23.   What about the people who eat a good diet and get sick? Once again, there are multiple factors: attitude and states of mind (fear, anger, shame, guilt and overwhelm weaken the body and mind), genes, assimilation ('we are what we assimilate', not what we eat), exposure to toxins, sedentary lifestyles, trauma, persistent stress, and more.

24.   And what about all the different groups claiming that their diet generates healing/is the best? You can see that I am inspired by the (raw) plant food diet, but I would like to share here the words of Zach Bush MD: *"Broadly speaking. I believe that there are two food categories: real food and processed food. I celebrate any education or diet that moves consumers toward real food. While I have long taught and practised a plant-based diet, I have never been dogmatic or judgemental toward alternative real food approaches. I recognize how continued infighting over narrower and narrower differences in the real food movement have kept us from successfully overcoming the processed food juggernaut. Let's topple the chemical companies and pharmaceutical mindset before we turn our collective energy toward sorting out the scientific truths in the real food factions."*

25.   When we turn to a cleaner, more energetically alive raw-fruit-and-greens diet, we are likely to experience detoxification as the body is now able to eliminate wastes. This can be uncomfortable, especially if the diet

has been rich in foods that have an acidic effect. It is wise to seek the assistance of a detox specialist when making big changes to one's diet.

26. It can also be helpful to interrupt set patterns and habits by going away on a holiday or retreat while learning to nurture, nourish and heal oneself.

27. Instead of giving your power away to the distant inventors of pharmaceuticals (who do not personally care about you, and stand to gain financially), discover what is possible for you by eating more raw fruits and vegetables. Look for the practitioners who actually reverse disease, restore health and regenerate the body. They are not miracle-workers; they are simply people who understand the laws of nature.

28. The body was designed to self-heal, given the right inputs and support.

WISDOM OF THE ANCIENTS

Hippocrates

"Primum non nocerum. (First do no harm.)"

"Natural forces within us are the true healers of disease."

"Before you heal someone, ask him if he is willing to give up the things that make him sick."

"All disease begins in the gut."

"Let food be thy medicine and medicine be thy food."

Desiderius Erasmus

"Prevention is better than cure."

The Mind and Emotions – Mind, Body, Spirit

In many cases illness is created by a poor diet, in which case changing the diet is a powerful way to restore health. But a key factor in our state of health is our emotions.

Our dominant thoughts and emotions establish a 'climate' and affect the tissue of our bodies: if we are often worried or angry, we are bathing ourselves in negative emotions that have a toxic effect on the body; if we are often optimistic and grateful, we are bathing ourselves in mostly positive emotions that have a calming and healing effect.

It's perfectly natural and normal to experience a balance of positive and negative thoughts and positive and negative emotions. It's not possible to be perpetually happy because life presents us with challenges and disappointments – that's how we grow. It's not even desirable to be perpetually happy because we need contrasting emotions – we wouldn't appreciate happiness if we didn't also experience sadness.

Seeking a perspective that encourages us, that makes us feel optimistic and open to others and to life, is the best way to transform challenging situations – it will be very beneficial to our physical health also.

In the case of trauma, which loads some people with far greater challenges than others experience, it is wise to reach out for help. There are many different services available.

In the meantime, some of the ideas in this story may provide useful perspectives for you.

- Reactors react to appearances.

• Creators create their desired experiences.

• Appearances are very seductive.
• Reacting is easy.
• Focused creation takes much more energy.

• You don't fight darkness; you turn on the light.
• What you resist, persists. The more you fight it, the stronger it gets.
• Self-rejection compounds darkness.

• Things don't exist until you measure (observe) them = events are neutral until we give them meaning.

• Love transforms.
• Everything is love.

• Everything is light, of different frequencies.

• Look in the mirror. If something 'out there' upsets you, find that same trait in you.
• Own it and appreciate it.

• Appreciate every event. Look for the blessings in how it *is*.
• Take responsibility for what you want to create.
• What, why, then how.

• If you lose focus on what you want to Create, you can easily fall back into Reaction. Just choose again.

• You will be tested many times...

• With love, gratitude, enthusiasm and focus, you will dissolve your problems and realise your dreams.
• Create on the inside first.

You, Mage.

The Next (current) War

"We are truly in a war. It is not the war we imagine we are in, which is the way our true adversaries want it. It is not a foreign war against a foreign enemy. It is a war on consciousness, a war on our own minds."
– Paul Levy

It is no longer possible to fight 'the enemy' with physical weapons: whoever has the greater or more sophisticated arsenal of weapons will win. The science fiction scenarios described in films like *Star Wars* (Artificial Intelligence and robot armies) and *The Omega Man* (pandemics as bioweapons) are today realistic scenarios.

Consequently, any major conflict can no longer be won by force. The 'worthy opponent' simply has too much physical and political power, even if that opponent only comprises 1% of the population. How, then, do the relatively unarmed ever vanquish their enemy?

Not by revolution, but by revelation.

By the power of the light.

By enlightened thinking and behaviour.

By responding to attack with love, poise and intelligence.

The response of love, poise and intelligence might not be easy, but it is possible.

If this sounds absurd to you, consider that a 'miracle' is simply the effect of a higher law.

Criminal activity is a reaction to disempowerment, and punishment is a reaction to criminal activity, but when the number of meditators in a particular region reaches a critical number, violent crime in those areas decreases.

This outcome looks like a miracle but it's simply the consequence of applying a higher law. Meditation has a stress-reducing and coherence-creating effect on individuals and society at large. Meditation is a higher law (= more enlightened response) than criminal activity.

Studies suggest there are underlying connections between individuals, and that a large enough group practising meditation will generate an extended 'field-like' effect in society. (The studies into this phenomenon demonstrate a significant result, not a random result. Eg. A study conducted between July 2006 and January 2007 by Maharishi University of Management in Fairfield Iowa.)

Just as only 1% of the population might be mal-intentioned but have the capacity to influence the other 99%, studies like the one mentioned above indicate that we only need 1% of the population meditating to see a significant effect. Imagine if even more people were to apply this higher law... What would happen to the so-called enemy's power?

This is a balanced universe: every positive is balanced by a negative, every particle by an anti-particle. There is no such thing as pure evil or pure good, as the yin/yang symbol reveals: light holds the potential for darkness and darkness holds the potential for light. Our 'enemy' is therefore also our ally, a 'worthy opponent': enemies challenge us to develop ourselves beyond what we might achieve in comfortable times.

Which brings us to one of the most transformational states of mind that exists: appreciation. When we consistently look for how a challenging experience serves us, we activate an emotional frequency, or vibration, of love and gratitude. This enlightened state of mind *is* a higher law...

"The only thing we have to fear is fear itself."
– Franklin D. Roosevelt

20% of the profit from each sale of this book will be donated to Farmer's Footprint, a coalition of farmers, educators, doctors, scientists, and business leaders aiming to expose the human and environmental impacts of chemical farming and offer a path forward through regenerative agricultural practices. Learn more: https://farmersfootprint.us/watch

"I cannot turn the tide in my clinics. I can't shift the momentum by working with one cancer patient at a time. It's far too slow and it's not at the root of the cause. And so I looked to farmers to realise the salvation of human health."
– Dr Zach Bush

"In 1965 4% of our population had a chronic disease. Today 46% of our children have a chronic disease."
– Dr Zach Bush

**If you've ever wondered what you can do to support human and Earth health, buying copies of this book is one way that you can contribute.
Available from www.lilianegrace.com/store**

The problem: *A century of monocrop farming and reliance on pesticides has damaged once-fertile soils and human health. The rapid increase in pesticide use over the past few decades has coincided with this explosion of chronic disease. Independent research from private laboratories and universities around the world are implicating glyphosate – the active ingredient in the herbicide Roundup.*

The solution: *Regenerative agriculture focuses on rebuilding organic matter and living biodiversity in soil, which produces increasingly nutrient-dense food year after year — while rapidly sequestering excess atmospheric carbon underground to reverse climate change.*

It brings proven results for farmers to have a profitable business and livelihood. Conventional inputs become unnecessary, increased organic matter in the soil brings insect biodiversity which helps manage pest pressure, and the end market for organic crops increases the overall value of their crop, making product value the priority over the conventional method of purely valuing yield.

At a time when there are more farmer suicides and bankruptcies than ever, bringing back economic success and life on the farm has never been more important.

Farmer's Footprint is the brainchild of Zach Bush MD, a physician specializing in internal medicine, endocrinology and hospice care. He is an internationally recognized educator and thought leader on the microbiome as it relates to health, disease, and our food production systems.

Dr Zach founded *Seraphic Group and the non-profit Farmer's Footprint to develop root-cause solutions for human and ecological health. His passion for education reaches across many disciplines, including topics such as the role of soil and water ecosystems in human genomics, immunity, and gut/brain health. His education has highlighted the need for a radical departure from chemical farming and pharmacy, and his ongoing efforts are providing a path for consumers, farmers, and mega-industries to work together for a healthy, regenerative future for the planet and our children.

https://.zachbushmd.com/
https://farmersfootprint.us/

Also by Liliane Grace...

The Mastery Club

Five twelve-year-olds form a club to support
each other in achieving their goals and dreams.
This personal development novel is packed with
practical tools and information about goal-setting,
constructive thinking, how the mind works, and
character values like persistence, courage and a
good attitude.

The Hidden Order

Inspired by the success of her goal-setting and
visualising efforts of last year, Natalie is determined
to keep the Mastery Club going, but the challenges
are stacking up: Nina has returned to her country life
and home education, Clare is starting at a new school
where she doesn't know anyone, Billy looks like he's
about to give up on the Club to get serious about sport,
and Sandy, as usual, is ready to argue with every one of
Nina's crazy but beautiful ideas.

Quest For Riches

Discover the four 'money personality types'
(which one are you?) as teenagers Toni, Eric,
Jackson and Brooke attempt to raise funds
for a school-organised trip to India. They get
there (one way or another), and are stimulated,
overwhelmed, discomfited and delighted by
the colourful and very different country of India.

Wanted: Greener Grass
— a novel about love, envy, and a crazy kind of courage

Mia and John's relationship has became flat and boring and she's over her job, so when John heads overseas for his father's funeral she feels relieved and excited and ready to explore new options.
'Conscious chick-lit'!

The Champion Series

Book One: The Boy Who Barked
Designed to inspire! About the life of Dr John Demartini, prolific author and international educator. A 44-page, full-colour picture book.

Book Two: The Boy Who Found His Pulse
Designed to inspire! About the life of Don Tolman, the Indiana Jones of wholefoods! A 44-page, full-colour picture book.

www.lilianegrace.com/store

About the Author

Liliane Grace specialises in empowering fiction, stories for children and adults that inspire and educate. A 10-week program based on her signature novel, The Mastery Club®, is available for students and families. She also teaches Creative Writing classes, offers a writing coaching and editing service, and is available to speak at your next event.

For more information about Liliane's books, programs and services, visit https://lilianegrace.com/

www.ingramcontent.com/pod-product-compliance
Lightning Source LLC
Chambersburg PA
CBHW010543100726
47903CB00011B/3122